FIGHTING FOR LOVE

D1521429

A Novel By
IRISH
LAHCHYNA

Contains explicit language & adult themes suitable for ages 16+

Remember….

You haven't read 'til you've read #Royalty

Check us out at

www.royaltypublishinghouse.com

Royalty drops #dopebooks

I dedicate this book to two people that have loving hearts and God's gift to help others.

Rebecca "Mommie" Atkinson
And
Teresa "Reet" Weeks- Davis
Rest in Heaven till we meet again
Your legacies live on.

IRISH LAHCHYNA

Chapter 1

(Palace – At the house)

Prince, Princess, Pierre, and I got up to ready ourselves for school. Our grandmother was always loud in the morning, yelling throughout the house.

"I know y'all asses heard me so get up before I get my switch and make y'all get up!" Grandmother said, poking her head inside our room.

"Palace, don't use all the hot water in the bathroom. I know how you do Palace, there are other people that have to go school besides you," my sister, Princess yelled at me.

Living in a three bedroom apartment with my granny was not the traditional household. I had to share a bedroom with my brothers, and sister. Princess and Prince were eighteen and they were getting ready to start their freshman year at FSU (Florida State University). My grandma was more than happy to get my brother and sister out the house.

"Yes, yes, yes Lord I thank you. Two more to go and I will have my house all to myself," Grandma would yelling throughout the house.

I finished taking my shower ready to start my senior year of high school.

"Dag, Palace, you took forever. I hope you didn't use all the hot water."

"No, Princess. I didn't use all the hot water. I'm just ready to get this year over with already."

"I hear you, little sister. Look, even though I'm leaving today doesn't mean anything. I'm still in Florida, I just want you to know I'm just one phone call away. I love Grandma and all but I won't be coming over this muthafucker like that. I'm ready to go than she is, trust me on that. I love ya little sis, and don't let this shit with Ma stress you the fuck out," she finished her speech, and then gave me a kiss before heading into the bathroom.

IRISH LAHCHYNA

When my sister said something about my mother, it hit a soft spot in my heart. I'd been trying not to think about my mother. When my brothers, sister and I were little, my mother was a grade A single parent. Our father, Prince Sr., left after Pierre's first birthday party. He said he was going to get some decorations and never came back. Word around town was my dad had another family in Jamaica. When we all got in high school, everything changed. It was my sophomore year, Pierre's freshman, and the twins' junior year. My mother got hooked on drugs. She would be gone days at a time, and sometimes even weeks. Whenever she came back, she would act like she'd only been gone an hour or two. For example, she would leave on Wednesday, at noon. She would come back two Wednesdays later at three in the afternoon. "I told y'all that would not take long, it's only three o'clock. Y'all know how Walmart is always packed! I couldn't move in there!" Mom would say.

I was a momma's girl all the way around, and I missed my mom. Things weren't the same at home anymore since she left, and I had a feeling things could get worse.

"Palace, let's go. The bus is coming!" Pierre yelled at me, snatching me out of my thoughts.

I gathered my things and ran to the bus stop.

Chapter 2

(Palace – First day of my senior year)

I walked in school with Pierre right on my tracks. I couldn't wait to get my year started as a senior. This was the last year I would be seeing Killian Senior High School and I could not wait to walk across the stage.

"Palace, I'm out. I got to catch up with Greg and Jamal in class. I love you Sis, and don't forget I have football practice today so I won't be on the bus," Pierre reminded me.

My little bro had grown up so much it scared me. My brother was 6'2, with short dreads in his hair. He was just starting his journey into locking his hair. I never wanted my brother to be a statistic in the system so I was against the dreads thing at first. I soon began to research the meaning of locs and learned it was purification to some cultures. That made feel better about him growing them. Maybe he was thinking it was just pure for him and not following the others' lead. My brother was the running back for our school and the thots were on him 24/7. My brother wasn't giving them any attention, and that was a good thing. Pierre wanted to be focused on his studies and football. His dream was to become a professional football player and I had a feeling one day soon, he would get his chance.

We stayed in the Pork and Bean projects, and every day there was always something going on. There was always shooting, fussing, cussing, robbing, fighting, killing. You name it, it was there. I wanted more out life and so did my sister and brothers.

"Palace, girl, what's up, girl?" my bestie Shuntae yelled as she approached me.

"Hey, Bestie! What's up with you? I thought you told me that you were wearing black and red today? It looks like you have on pink and black to me."

"I know, girl. I was but when I started looking in my closet, I wanted to wear this. Don't be mad at me. I see you have on your black and red, though. It looks good on you," Shuntae said

"Yeah, whatever. Let's go to class."

"Palace, what you mean, class? You mean breakfast then auditorium, right?"

"Shuntae, girl, I forgot all about breakfast," I started laughing as we headed to the cafeteria.

I hated school food but we always had the bomb ass pizzas and nachos with cheese. When we had those, my face was definitely in the place. Shuntae and I got in the line to get our food. This morning they had the french toast sticks or Pop Tarts with eggs or grits. We got french toast sticks, grits, and orange juice.

We headed to our seats. We'd sat in the same spot for three years straight and we weren't trying to change now. As we walked up, I saw the rest of my girls waiting for Shuntae and me.

"What's up, ladies?" Nicole said

"Hey Nicole, hey Brooke! What's going on with you?" I said to my girls.

Nicole started to run me the gossip immediately. "Palace, girl, Brooke already starting her day off wrong. She and Peanut fussing early this morning about him looking at some girl's butt."

Brooke was my girl, but she was so clingy to Peanut it was crazy. Peanut was my brother's friend, Jamal. He was a senior but they had been friends what seemed like forever. Brooke and Peanut had been together since freshman year. The first two years were good. I wanted a relationship like theirs. They had the kind of relationship that made you want to say, "Fuck it, let's just go to the justice of peace now" type situation. That was until we got in our junior year. It was prom season and the crew really wasn't feeling it. We'd decided that on prom night, we would just chill with each other with whoever we was with.

Well, on the night of prom, Peanut told Brooke that he wasn't feeling well, so he decided to stay home for the night. The next day, we went to the mall. As we were coming out of the Nike store, we saw Fatima going into the store with her get-along gang.

"Damn, bitch, when you see me, you need to move the fuck out of my way," Fatima said as she looked dead at Brooke.

Brooke looked at her and burst out laughing. "Bitch, you wish I would. Fatima, get the fuck on. Ain't nobody got time for your fucking mouth today."

"You may not have time for my mouth but Peanut sure does. Ask him about what we did after the prom last night."

"Nah, bitch. Since you so good with running your mouth, why don't you tell me?"

"Brooke, girl, you ain't even worth the pleasure, but I will tell you this. Peanut has one sexy ass birth mark on his right butt cheek."

In the blink of an eye, we were all throwing punches and we all got kicked out of the mall.

Since then, Brooke took him back, and let's just say that they haven't been the same since. She didn't trust him any further than she could see him. She was on him like white on rice and it wasn't a good thing. She wouldn't really hang with us anymore because she went wherever he went. That shit was embarrassing.

"Y'all ready? Let's head to the auditorium," Shuntae said.

We all got up to start our first day of our senior year.

Chapter 3

(Palace – What a day, what a day.)

The auditorium was packed. I saw the some of the same faces from the years before, with the new freshmen class. I usually thought this part was boring but being this is my last year, I was hyped. I looked up and saw my brother and his football squad enter the auditorium. The girls were whistling and shit, trying to get my brother's attention. Little did they know, he wasn't hearing them.

Principal Hayes grabbed the microphone to quiet us down so she could get the assembly started. "Quiet down, quiet down, everyone so we can get this started, and everyone can enjoy their first day of class!" Principal Hayes yelled for everyone to hear.

The assembly lasted for two hours and half of the day was already gone. My girls and I had third lunch. I could not wait to get to the cafeteria to chit chat and see what's new.

I walked in the cafeteria and my stomach started to growl. I didn't think I was that hungry but I guess my stomach felt otherwise. I didn't know what we were having, but I'm praying that it was something that I could digest. If not, I would be going hungry today. Luckily they had pizza! I grabbed two slices and my milk then headed to our table.

"Damn, chick. It took you ass long enough! Where have you been?" Shuntae quizzed.

"Girl, I had gym class and I had to change my clothes. What did I miss?"

"Shit, we're just looking to see who is new and trying to find out the latest gossip."

I hate to admit it, but lunch was boring for the first day of school. It was always hyped for first day. We chopped it a little bit then we talked about hooking up later to walk around.

"How was your first day, baby girl?" my grandmother greeted me as soon as I walked in the door.

"It was good, Grandma, but it was boring."

"Really, that's a first. I wonder why it was so boring."

I heard stuff being shuffled in my mother's room. I looked up at my grandmother and knew exactly why she was holding a conversation with me. She didn't want me know that my mother was here. I walked in my mother's room and was stuff everywhere.

"Ma, what are you doing in here?"

"Hey, baby. I didn't see you standing there, Palace."

I looked long and hard at my mother. The clothes she had on reeked and she looked like she hadn't washed in days. My mom didn't look like herself, and I couldn't understand how she even got to this point her life.

"Ma, what is going on with you, and why do you look like a homeless woman that's been out in the streets for days and days?"

"Palace, sit down for a minute. Let me talk to you."

As soon as I sat down, my mom sat down beside me and started looking me up and down. Before I knew it, my mother jumped on top of me and started yelling at me. "I KNOW YOU GOT SOME MONEY, PALACE!!! LET ME FEEL YOUR POCKETS!!!"

I was shocked and scared at the same time. It was like a demon had gotten into my mother or something. I pushed her off of me and was about to give her the business. My grandmother grabbed my hand as soon as I pulled it back to slap my mom.

"Palace, stop what you're doing and go for a walk now!"

I started to say something but my grandmother held up her hand for me not to even speak. I looked down at my mother. She was balled up in the corner like she was scared. I couldn't wrap my head around what had just taken place. My mother attacked me but she was in a corner like I attacked her.

I ran out the door with tears in my eyes. Everyone was outside and, living in the projects, everyone was nosey. I started running and didn't have a clue to where. I needed to vent. I could not vent to anyone in the house, nor talk to these nosey ass people around here.

I ran until I was almost out of breath. I realized I made it to Queens Street. It wasn't as bad as the projects but it had its faults. The neighborhood was okay and the houses actually looked decent. I would rather live here than in the Pork and Beans. I heard some commotion coming from the side of a house. The voice sounded so familiar so I wanted to see if my ears were hearing right.

I peeked around the corner and I saw my baby brother, Pierre, arguing with some dope boy. When I looked down, he had something in his hand, so I assumed it was some dope. As soon as he saw me, he ran. I could not believe my brother, but the dope boy standing before me was fine as hell.

Chapter 4

(Squeeze – The meet up, maybe a new beginning or mistake)

I was about to go after Pierre about my money until I turned around and saw shorty in front of me. The girl before me was not a hoodrat from the projects, she looked to be the just the total opposite. She was thick, and I like my women thick. Her caramel complexion and her hair was cut in razor bob had me drooling from the mouth. I was going to get up with Pierre later but right now I wanted to get to know the fine woman standing before me.

"Hey, how are you? My name is Squeeze, and may I ask to know your name?"

She looked at me like she had attitude with me or something. She was mean mugging me hard but that shit was turning a nigga on. "What is this, fuck up Palace's day? What the fuck, man? I can't catch a fucking break!" she replied.

Ole girl was screaming with her hands in the air. I thought she was losing it, and I was about to back the fuck up. She was cute and all but I didn't deal with crazy people. Before I was getting ready to head to my whip, something told me to turn back around.

I turned around and she was on her knees crying her eyes out. I didn't know what drew me to her but I went and helped her up from the ground. As soon as she was up on her feet, she embraced me with a loving hug.

"Look, I don't know you but my name is Palace. Can you please take me take the fuck away from here, please?"

I looked at her and I took her to my spot on the East Side. She didn't say anything on the way to my crib, she just looked out the window. When we pulled up to my crib, she got out with her head down and tear stains on her cheeks.

"Who house is this?" Her voice was soft like a baby's.

"This my house, shorty. Come on in. I'm not going to bite."

Soon as I opened the door, she walked in like she'd been at my spot before. She took a seat on my living room couch. While I was getting myself together, I had to admire her beauty. She had dimples in both cheeks. Whether she smiled or not, the print was very visible.

"Look, Squeeze, I hope I'm not intruding and I hope your girlfriend won't be upset that I'm here."

"Nah, you good, boo. I don't do the relationship thing so you ain't got nothing to worry about."

Chapter 5

(Palace – This a feeling I never felt)

I had to admit, for Squeeze to be single, his taste in decorations was flattering. His house was full African art, Black artifacts, and I loved how he had it laid out. In the center of his floor was a lion rug with the head still attached! On the right wall of his living room was a huge picture of Nefertiti. On the left wall was a huge portrait of Maya Angelou with her writing on a piece of notebook paper. I love Maya Angelou. Her poems and captivating words got me through a lot of bad days. In the center of his wall, mounted over his fireplace, was a picture of Martin Luther King Jr, Malcolm X, and President Barack Obama. They were all holding hands like they were leading a march. His place spoke volumes and was masculine in its own way. It was like he demanded power, and power from a wise Black man nowadays was a plus in my book.

I got up and walked toward Squeeze as he was sitting on a bar stool in his kitchen. I was looking at this man and he was sexy as hell. His dreads hung past his shoulders to the middle of his back, with the tips dyed auburn. He was built like the rapper, Ace Hood. His caramel skin along with all his tattoos had my panties moist.

I had to get my head together. How could I want a man that was helping destroy the Earth by poisoning our people with crack rocks, powder, and whatever else he was selling? I knew he wasn't for me but right now I just wanted to get some of the stress off of me. I wanted this man inside of me in the worst way.

He stood up and I finally noticed how tall this man was. He had to be at least 6'2. His height and sexy body had me in heat. I didn't know what came over me but I grabbed him by his neck, trying to pull him to me. I wanted to feel his lips against mine. I was so ready for that touch until I felt him pulling back from me.

"Aye, shorty, slow your roll. I ain't looking for all that, ma."

I felt so embarrassed at what I had just done and more so that he'd rejected me. I couldn't even pick my face up off the floor because it had fallen six feet under from the embarrassing state I was in. I moved back to the living room and sat back on the couch I was on before.

"Hey, can I have something to drink, if you don't mind?" I asked him

"What would you like? I have soda, juice, beer, Grey Goose, Hennessy, and some Beefeater."

I needed something real strong to take some of my pain away, and since I couldn't get Squeeze inside of me to take it away, I went for something bad.

"I will take Grey Goose with orange juice"

"Okay, I will bring it to you. That shit sounds nasty but I'm going to try one with you because I think we both need a drink."

After thirty minutes of indulging in our drinks, I was feeling lovely. We started a real conversation and I found his real name was Dontrae Thomas. He got the nickname Squeeze because he caught his first body when he was nine. He was at home with his mother and brothers when one of his mother's many boyfriends decided to drop by. He came in the house demanding sex from his mom and she wasn't really having it. She asked the man to leave but he just kept on feeling on his mother. Dontrae got tired of seeing his mother fight with the man, so Squeeze went in his older brother's room and got his gun. He went back to the living room where the man was still fumbling with his mother and shot him dead in the head. He was smiling after he squeezed the trigger and that became his nickname.

I was feeling lovely and so was he. Before I knew it, our clothes were coming off. I was as naked as day I came in this world. I wasn't a virgin. I'd had sex twice in my life but those guys were nothing compared to the monster that was hanging between Squeeze's legs.

My mouth was drooling. I really didn't know a thing about sucking a man's dick but for some reason, I wanted him in my mouth. He grabbed me and kissed me, starting at my mouth to going down to my hips. I thought he was going to eat my pie but boy, I was fooled. He turned me over and my sweetness was soaked in my own nectar. Squeeze entered me with his masculine shaft and I was loving every thrust as he was pumping in and out of me. This wasn't a love session but it was taking me to high places, and all my stress was fading away.

I never knew that a fuck session could take away the pain I was feeling but it did, and I was grateful to Squeeze for that.

Chapter 6

(Squeeze – Well damn)

My body felt drained as I began shift in my bed. I tried to lift up my head and it felt like a ton of bricks. I had a bad hangover. I also just remembered I had this girl here with me.

I got up, grabbed some clothes, and headed to the bathroom to handle my hygiene. After that, I went into the kitchen to get my coffee started. I noticed that my house was quiet, and ole girl was nowhere in sight. My mind started to wonder where she had gone. I checked every room, and I even called out her name but all I got was silence.

Damn, how could I be so fucking stupid? I didn't strap up with shorty and I didn't know her from Eve. That's why I liked to drink by myself in the comfort in my own home. It seemed like whenever I drank with other people, I always got myself in a situation. I hoped she was on birth control and I had to get to my doctor like ASAP.

I pulled out my cell to call my doctor's office and set up an appointment but my phone started ringing before I could make my call. I looked at the caller ID and it was my oldest brother Tres.

"What's up, brah?"

"Not shit, Squeeze. I had to call you to let you know that Grandma and Ma having a cookout today at the house."

"Oh word, what's the occasion?"

"I don't know but Grandma wants us all together, and she said you can bring whoever you want."

"Alright, man. I will be through later. Tell Nanna I love her and I will see her then. Tres, how shit looking over there?"

"Squeeze, you know better than to ask me what you know. I hold shit down on my side."

I had to laugh at my brother. I knew me asking him that question would get under his skin.

We hung up the phone and I was trying to figure out why Nanna wanted us all together for a cookout. My mom and I didn't get along at all because I didn't agree with her job profession. My mother, Sarafenia, is a forty-five year old stripper. She was mature in age, but if you didn't know her, you have sworn she was about seventeen. She kept her body tight by going to the gym but it was like her skin wasn't aging at all. Who wants to see their mother on a pole shaking what God gave her? To make matters worse, she was a grandmother. Both my brothers had kids. Tres had two girls, Tyrin, who was three years old, and Tiana, she's one year old. My brother Kareme had a son named, King, who was one year old, and a baby on the way by his wife Kahsay.

I grabbed my coffee, called my doctor and headed to his office.

Chapter 7

(Pierre - Everything isn't always what it seems)

I wasn't expecting to run into my sister tonight. I was chopping it up with Squeeze about some things I needed to handle. I was tired of the environment that I was living in and I wanted a come up for a better life.

When I walked up to the house, I saw my so-called mother sitting on the porch. I didn't want to speak to her. I was just going to walk past her until she stopped me.

"Pierre, you don't see me sitting here?"

"Ma, I see you but that don't mean much. I look at you with sympathy in my heart, and it hurts, Ma. I go to school and my friends tell me how they see you coming out of crack houses. I get joked on and laughed at all the time. Ma, you just don't understand, do you? The sad thing about it is you probably never will."

My mother could not even look at me. The shame was written all on her face. I walked in the door and saw Grandma was in the kitchen cooking.

"Hey, Era, did you see your sister out there? Palace and your momma had a fight, and I told her to leave to cool off. Palace ran out of here like a bat out of hell."

Era was my nickname, and that's what everyone called me around the hood.

"No, Grandma. I didn't see her out in the projects. What was the fight about, and why did you ask Palace to leave?"

"Era, that girl was about to strike your momma, and you know I don't play that."

"Ma must have done something to Palace to make her take it there. It takes a lot for Palace to get mad, Grandma, and you know that."

"I know but regardless, that's her mother and she should never go against her mother. I know all of you are mad at your mother but you have to understand that she has an illness. I don't know what happened to my baby, but I pray for her soul every night the devil will let go of her."

"I love you, Grandma. I'm going to bed. I have practice tomorrow and I'm tired. I'm not mad at her, I'm just disappointed in her. Right now, all we can do is pray for her and her soul."

I hated to lie to Grandma about seeing Palace, but if I didn't, I would have had to explain why I was on that side of town. I didn't know why Palace was over there but I would find out in the morning on our way to school.

***

When I woke up the next morning, I called Palace's name and to my surprise, I didn't get an answer. I was wondering where she was and why she wasn't at home.

Between her seeing me last night with Squeeze and her getting into it with Ma, I didn't know what I was going to say to Palace. There was no telling what my sister was going through right now but I hoped and prayed she was safe out there. My mind got the best of me so I decided to hit up her cell. I dialed her number again and it went straight to voicemail.

"Aye, Era, come on. The bus is coming soon!" Jamel yelled through the door

I ran into the bathroom to handle my hygiene and got dressed for school.

Chapter 8

(Paris – They will never know my pain)

My mind was wandering in every direction. I loved my kids more than they would never know. I had accepted the fact that I fell off has a mother but I would never allow my kids to strike me. I saw Palace and I wanted to hug her and let her know that I was okay but the urge took over. I wanted a hit and I had to get one any way I knew how.

Some months back, I had seen the love of my life with another woman. Prince left me on Pierre's first birthday. We had our share of problems but no relationship was perfect. I never thought he would actually leave me and his children. The fact that he was still in Miami after all these years had me in pain.

I couldn't tell my kids that I saw their father and didn't have the nerve to approach him. They would ask all kinds of questions and I didn't have an answer to give them. I was proud of my children but slumped in my own fear. My twins were off to college, and I didn't even see them off on their special day. This was Palace's last year in high school, and I couldn't even pick myself up to be there for her.

My days consisted of watching Prince Sr. and his little whore around town. I always had to be high to even look at him. Pierre was right, I would go the neighborhood drug houses just to get a hit. I would see children my kids' ages all the time around those houses. I didn't care what they saw or even the fact that they knew my kids. All I wanted was to get high.

I got twenty dollars out my mom's pocketbook after the little scuffle between Palace and I. I was looking at the money and I was ready to get another hit. When I sat down on the porch, the breeze I was feeling felt so good, so I just sat there for a while.

I was thinking about Prince Sr. I knew I needed to clean myself up in order to get him back. I looked at the twenty dollars and told myself, *I'm done after tonight. Just one last hit.*

I got up to go search for my next high.

Chapter 9

(Palace – Just thinking, just thinking)

I woke up, looked over at Squeeze, and immediately felt bad. I wasn't a thot or some hoe in the streets but I'd just slept with a man I don't even know. I looked at his sleepy face. He was sleeping so peacefully.

I quietly got my naked butt up and went in the living room to collect my clothes. I gathered my clothes up and then went inside the hall bathroom to handle my hygiene. I found a wash cloth on a shelf he had custom built. I was glad he had some Dove soap because I didn't want to walk around smelling like a man. I had on the same clothes that I had on yesterday so I knew I had to get ghost. I didn't want to go home because I felt kind of awkward after seeing Pierre and having a fight with my mom. I turned my cell on and it was jumping with text messages and voicemails.

I knew I should be on the way to school but shit, I'd had one hell of night and really didn't want to go. My phone started vibrating in my hand and I saw that my bestie was hitting me up.

"Hello?"

"Damn, bitch, it's like that now? I been calling your ass all night! You good, boo?"

"Shuntae, damn, quit hollering in my damn ear. I'm good, where you at?"

"Palace, do you see what time it is, honey? It's going on ten o'clock. You know where my ass is at. I'm somewhere you're supposed to be... School!"

Ten o'clock? Well damn, I can't go over her house. So I guess I have to go home.

"Alright, Shuntae, damn. Call me when you get out of school so we can meet up."

"Nah, heifer. You said that shit yesterday and your ass was a no-show. I'm not calling you. I will be at your house so you need to be in place, ma'am," Shuntae told me and hung up the phone.

Damn, I hated that I had to go back to the crib but I guess I needed go to see what was going to happen anyway.

I pulled out my key and unlocked the door. My grandma was in her favorite chair watching re-runs of *The Cosby Show*. I went straight to my room and didn't say a word to her. I pulled off my clothes and for some reason, I wanted to bathe again. I grabbed towel, wrapped it around me and was headed to the bathroom. As soon as I got in the hallway, my granny stopped me.

"Palace, come in the living room. We need to talk. Now!"

I should have known better than to think I can could come in and my granny would not say a thing to me. "Yes, ma'am."

"Palace, I sent you out of here last night so you could cool down. I didn't think you would stay out all night! Anyway, listen to me, Palace. I know your mother ain't the best but it all remains the same, she is your mother. I will never allow any of my kids to do so much as raise their voice at me, let alone raise their hand to strike me. I know your mother made you angry but baby girl, ain't nothing good going to come to you if you disobey your mother."

"Grandma, I know. I let my anger take control of me, and I apologize for my actions."

"Good, good. I taught you, well girl. I love you, Palace, and you are grown but don't you be bringing no great grandbabies in here."

"That's one thing you don't have to worry about. I don't want any kids. I would rather wait."

"Okay, go take a shower, you got your coochie juice all on my chair, girl"

I had to laugh at Grandma, she always knew how to make me smile, even on a bad day.

Chapter 10

(Shuntae – That's my best friend, that's my best friend)

I was in my last class for the day and I couldn't figure out why the hell my bestie wasn't here. I'd called her phone all yesterday because we were supposed to hook up. I called and called. First, it was just ringing then it started going straight to voicemail. I waited an hour, then I called back, and homegirl had just turned off her phone.

Palace and I had been hella close since the day she'd moved into Pork and Beans. In these projects, you had to be ready for anything with these hating ass females around here. These girls around this way were always ready to fight, and it was never one-on-one. They liked to jump around here. Granny, Palace's grandmother, was really like the grandmother to the Beans. I mean, she would set our asses straight and she didn't tolerate disrespectful children that talked back to their parents.

I loved that lady with all my heart. I never got a chance to meet my granny so she was just as close to blood as it got. So when she told me that her grandchildren were moving in with her, I got hyped.

I had one brother named Mareese. He was twenty-eight and known around these parts as Danger. My brother had fear in everyone, no one fucked with him. That made my life hard. Being the sister of a well-known hustler had its perks but it had a bad downside. I mean yeah, I got respect in the streets but me having a relationship was dead. I could never get someone to have a relationship with me. I had a few dudes that were new to the scene, and I kept them in the dark about who my brother was. News in the Beans traveled fast, though. I'd never had a real relationship before and I wanted one bad.

I had few dudes that would hit me off with the dick a couple times but that shit would be crazy. We could be in the middle of fucking then the paranoia started. They would act as if they just got finished hitting the stem or some shit. They would be hitting it from the back and be close to the window so they could peek out the curtains to see if my brother was coming. Sometimes they would jump if they heard noises. If they even thought they'd heard a noise, they would get up in the middle of our session and leave. That was some straight bullshit so I just said fuck the hood boys. I was hoping when I left and went to college I would find someone that wasn't scared of my brother.

The bell rang, making me dismiss my thoughts for that moment. I went out to catch my bus to go home. Riding on the bus was never not my cup of tea. Someone that was either musty or had bad breath that sat beside me. I just put in my Dollar General headphones to listen to my music from my cell and looked out the window.

We pulled up to my stop, and I hopped off headed straight to Palace's house. I knocked on the door and she let me in.

"So what's good, chick? Why weren't you at school?'

"Shuntae, I had a crazy night."

"Well, spill, bitch. Everything. I want to know it all."

Palace told me her story and I was blown away. Damn. I heard around the way that a boy named Squeeze's pockets were fat as hell. I thought that my girl should go for him. I mean, all our lives we were struggling, wearing hand-me-downs and all. I thought that since we would be leaving soon, we should do something better.

"Palace, why don't you want to see what ole boy talking about?"

"Shuntae, you know I don't get down like that and he wasn't my type anyway."

We got off that subject and started talking about other things.

"So, Palace, I was thinking that we could go do something to help out the community."

"Like what?"

"Okay, before you object to what I'm going to say, just hear me out, Palace."

We were poor but there were people out there doing way worse than us. Palace and I had a warm spot in our hearts for helping those less fortunate. When we saw people that needed spare change or something, we always gave them whatever we had.

"I was wondering if you'd go with me on the weekends to volunteer at the soup kitchen."

"Why are you going to a soup kitchen?"

"Every weekend they feed the homeless at the gym, and I think we should participate."

"Sure, that sounds like it would be fun. I'm down!"

I was so happy she said okay. I'd never been to a soup kitchen but helping others out was something we just loved to do.

Chapter 11

(Squeeze – Family affair)

I went straight to my doctor's office. I know I should've been more careful but that vodka had a brother feeling right. I'd never been in a female raw and wasn't ever planning on it unless she had my last name. I had to admit it felt so good and moist inside her.

I wanted to talk to ole girl some more to at least find out some things about her. Like, was she on some kind of birth control? I didn't get her number or anything, just a straight fuck session. I knew I was slipping, I needed to get back on my game. I couldn't get ole girl out of my mind, though. I wanted her in the worst way.

"Squeeze, Doctor Anderson is waiting for you."

Yes, even in the doctor's office they called me by my nickname. I prefered it that way.

"Thank you," I told the receptionist

"How're you doing, young man?"

"Well, Doc, I messed up last night. I went in a shorty raw and I don't know a thing about her."

"Young man, what were you thinking about? Never mind, don't answer that."

I had to laugh at Doctor Anderson, he was a mess but he always kept it real.

"You do know that it can take days to show up if something was transmitted between you and the young woman. Don't you?"

"I'm just scared. I'm not trying to catch nothing. I'm just like a woman, my body is my temple."

"Okay, we will take some blood work and run some STD tests for you. I advise from now on, you to think with your head on top of your shoulders rather than the one that's in between your legs."

"Yes sir, you got it."

Doctor Anderson walked out. Shortly after, I got my blood drawn. I forgot about the additional test that required a sample to be taken some from my private area. The nurse stopped me, so I had to get this test done. I knew I was definitely slipping now and I needed to get it together.

I walked into Grandmother's house and I immediately smelled food. I went to the backyard to find my granny, my brothers with some girls, and my mom with, I guess, her new sponsor for the week.

"Hey, my baby, did you bring me a soon-to-be granddaughter?" My grandmother always wanted me to settle down with someone but that's wasn't in my plan for now.

"Grandma, you know I don't want a relationship right now."

"Boy, if you don't get a girl soon, people are going to swear you're gay. Matter of fact, I'm starting think that myself."

"Y'all can think whatever y'all want. I know different so it don't matter what y'all think." I gave my grandma a kiss on her forehead and went to chop it up with my brothers and whoever they were with.

"Yo, brah, what it do?"

"Not shit. Who's the lady on your arm, man?" I asked Tres.

"Brah, this is one of my homegirls from around the way."

Homegirl was fine, and I knew I hadn't seen her in our neck of the woods before. I had to lick my lips because I swear I was about to drool all over myself. She was drop dead gorgeous. She was brown skinned with the prettiest hazel eyes I had ever seen. Her hair was long, like down to her ass long. It looked fake but when you got up close, you tell it was all hers.

"Hi, my name is Nicole, and yes, I'm just a friend."

"I'm Squeeze. Tres is my oldest brother. It is nice to meet you, Nicole."

Nicole was hella fine but it didn't take a rocket scientist to see that she had eyes for my brother. That's a line we don't cross. I look at Nicole and said damn, too bad for me because if she didn't have eyes for my brother, she could get the business.

My brother Kareme came and dapped me up and introduced me to Tarah, his girl's sister. Now this girl wasn't even my type but when she spoke to me, I was feeling her.

"Aye, Mon, my name is Tarah."

That Jamaican accent made up for her looks, I swear. A foreign girl with sexy accent as just pure sexy in my eyes. Tarah was high yellow, and I didn't do high yellow but I may make an exception this time. She had to be at least 5'1, I was 6'2, and she was short compared to me. Her dreads were in a high bun and she had green eyes. She had no ass but hella boobs.

"Aye, y'all come in the kitchen. Let your guests stay outside!" my grandma yelled from her back patio.

We all went in the kitchen. I looked at my mother in pure disgust. I could not understand why she liked the pole so much. She clearly was a beautiful woman inside and out. She was dressed in some black skinny jeans, a purple crop top and purple heels, dressed like she was going to work.

"This is a family gathering. You should've dressed more presentable," I scolded my mom. She just looked at me and rolled her eyes.

"I called y'all in here, and this family get-together so we could all talk." The look in my grandmother eyes let me know that it was something serious. "I want to expand our family business a little more. I want to open up two restaurants, one on the main strip, and one on the south side of the Beans."

Our family owned three group homes for kids, and five homeless shelters throughout Miami. My grandmother, Idella Mae, and grandfather Thomas started the shelters, and group homes in 1998. My grandfather made a living for his family working at a steel plant. My grandfather saved his money, while my grandmother took care of home with their three children in a one bedroom shack. He saved enough to build the house that we are in now, down to last brick.

My grandparents wanted better living for Blacks. They were tired of seeing women, children, and men that were homeless roaming the street. They gave the people their dollars, and spare change, and it helped a few. But that didn't satisfy their need to do more, so that's what they did.

"Grandma, that's a good idea. I'm down with that but who is going to manage them?"

"I'm glad you asked, my lovely grandson, because you are going to manage one of them."

"Grandma, I have my hands tied up as it is running the shelter on Main. Now you want me to do this. Why mom can't do it?"

"Look, son, I have faith in you. I would not dare expose my business dealings with your mom, she's shaking her tail for a quick buck."

"Hey, y'all talking like I'm not right here," my mom said and stormed off.

We all just looked at each other but my mom knew my grandmother didn't care for what she did for income. She didn't have to strip because our businesses kept us afloat. Plus, my grandfather left us wealthy. After my grandfather built this house, he got hurt at the steel plant. We later found out a white man set him up to get hurt because he was Black. Grandad sued the plant and won. Lucky for him, he had a good lawyer. He won three and a half million dollars in his case. So my mother made her choice to shake her ass, because she really didn't have to.

"So, Grandma, when this going to take place?"

"Your Uncle Ray and Slim are preparing the paperwork with the lawyers and everyone else. I need you to meet your uncles this week so you can put your name on the deed son."

"Grandma, what are you talking about, signing my name on a deed?"

"Son, this will be your restaurant. I'm giving you this like I gave your brothers and cousins some of the shelters and group homes. Your uncles did successfully expand so their children could benefit, and I don't mind. The more we have, the more we help, so it's all good," Grandmother said.

I got up and hugged my grandmother. She was one awesome woman. For her to be in her eighties, she didn't look a day over forty. I gave my grandmother kiss on her forehead and she kissed me on my cheek.

I felt a vibration in my pocket and I knew it was my phone so I checked to see who was calling me. It was a girl I'd met last weekend at Club Diamond. I shot her a text to let her know I would meet up with her later, knowing damn well that I was lying.

We left the kitchen to enjoy the rest of our family cookout.

Chapter 12

(Sarafenia – How could they understand the feeling I felt)

Shit! I had to go and get away from my mother's house ASAP. I was driving like a mad woman as Anthony, my little sponsor, was looking at me like I had two heads. He was enjoying himself while I was in my mom kitchen getting talked about like a dog. He was lusting over the two chicks my sons brought over.

"Nia?" Anthony called my name quietly.

"What!"

"Why the hell you screaming at me, Nia? It's not my fault you were in a rush to leave your parents' house."

Nia was my nickname because Sarafenia was too long for my liking.

"Anthony, I'm going to drop you off at your crib. I will come back to pick you up later."

"The hell you mean, drop me off? My truck is at your spot. You can take me to my truck. Then when you calm down, hit me up."

I was so heated, I forgot all about Anthony's truck. I pulled up to my crib, he got out and slammed my door. I watched him pull out of my driveway like a bat out of hell. At first I was going to go riding to clear my head, but I'd settle for taking a shot of Remy in my bed.

I walked into my four bedroom home. I had my place laid out in zebra print everything. I loved my house. I had three bathrooms, my kitchen was state of art, the house was Ikea furnished, had an indoor pool, and a Jacuzzi inside and out. My master bath was huge, with a huge built-in a shoe closet, and my clothes filled the 'His' and 'Her' closets.

I went straight to my alcohol cooler, pulled out the Remy and a shot glass. I tossed it back and felt the burn go down my throat. It was soothing and refreshing, and I had to have another one. I tossed that one back and was just as refreshing as the first one. Fuck it, I would just take the whole fucking bottle. Shots weren't going to give me the affect that I wanted.

No one understood how I felt. I had my kids early in my life. I was eighteen when I had my first child, Treston. I thought he would be my one and only until my six week checkup. I was pregnant again with Kareme, and two years later, I had Squeeze. I was supposed to be living life but I had to be shacked up with Jamal. Jamal was the boys' father and I was in love with him. He was a good father to my kids.

One day, I was supposed be working late and Jamal was watching our boys. I got off early. I would usually call and tell Jamal I was on my way home but something told me not to. When I arrived home, my boys were all in the living room watching T.V. My kids saw me at the door but I hushed them quickly so I could surprise Jamal. I made it to our bedroom door and I heard noises from the other side. I opened the door and I saw Jamal in the bed with my best friend Tammy getting it on. I rushed them while they were in their little love session. They didn't even see me coming. As soon as I got up on them, they had all kind of excuses. I didn't want to hear none of that bullshit they were saying.

I grabbed my children and put them I the car so they wouldn't see the damage I was about to do. I went back and grabbed my baseball bat. When I got back in, they were both fully dressed and trying to explain what happened. I swung the bat at him but he ducked, then I went for her. I was like hell nah, I don't need a bat for her because I'm gonna kill this bitch with my bare hands. The bitch had a nerve to start crying! I didn't what she was crying for because crying wasn't going to save her ass. I grabbed that bitch by her throat and started going in on her head. Tammy was gasping for air and Jamal was just standing there stuck for a moment, then he tried to get me off of her.

"Nia, baby, calm down. It's not what you think!"

That nigga must have thought I rode the slow bus or something because I actually knew what I saw. I started asking to myself if all this shit was I was doing was worth the fight. No.

So I went into the kitchen grabbed a few trash bags and did a complete sweep of everything he had. This nigga was on his knees trying to help Tammy to her feet. When he saw what I was doing, he dropped that bitch.

"Baby! What are doing, Nia?"

"What the hell does it look like, nigga? You must think I'm a stupid ass broad or something. Nigga, you getting the hell out of here!"

"Where the hell I'm supposed to go, Nia?"

"I don't know, Jamal. go stay with that bitch over there but it won't be here. I don't even know how either one of you are getting anywhere because that Altima out there belongs to me! So you may as well drop them keys and get to walking!"

By that time, he was literally begging me to let him stay, promising he would do right from now on. I wasn't trying to hear that shit. When I love, I love hard, and once you fuck that up, it's a wrap. I kindly grabbed the bags, tied them up, and put them on the curb by the trash can. I walked to the car, got my kids out the car and we walked back in as he stood outside with Tammy. He was trying to gather his things up and put them at front door. I closed the door and locked it. He wasn't getting back in here.

I hadn't seen Jamal since. I mean, aside from the couple of times that he came to get the boys but I ignored his presence, so that really didn't count. I was busy because my mother had me working in the shelters and the soup kitchen for years. Even though we had money, we had to earn money from our parents. They didn't want us to be raised like we never had to work.

After that night with Jamal, I was depressed. My heart turned cold toward all men and I didn't care to trust any broad like that. So I decided I would use men for my needs. As far as working the strip club, I did that because it gave me a sense of freedom. I worked, worked, worked, and took care of my kids in my younger days. Now that my kids were grown, my youth was now, and I was enjoying my life to the fullest.

Chapter 13

(Palace – so we meet again)

School was going great! I was passing all my classes. It had been almost two months since my little love session with Squeeze, and he had been on my mind heavy. My brother never told me what the deal was with him and Squeeze. He just assured me that it didn't have a thing to do with drugs. I just took him at his word because I knew my brother was smarter than that.

It was the weekend and I was ready to go help in the soup kitchen. Shuntae and I had been working here a month and a half, and we enjoyed every minute of it. I'd met a lot of people here. They shared their stories with me about how they got in the predicaments they were in. Just hearing their stories made want to do so much more but I didn't have the means of doing what I had in mind. I met a cutie named Markia. She was a volunteer and was about twelve years old. She loved to help others more than anyone I knew. She had a heart of gold and her soul was genuine to her beliefs. Markia was so gifted. She had her school, plus some of her friends from her neighborhood helping with the soup kitchen.

Ms. Idella, the lady that owned the building, made Shuntae and I feel like family. I really love her. She had so much passion for helping others that people call her the Mother Teresa of Miami.

"Hello, ladies, how is it going?"

"Hi, Ms. Idella!" Shuntae and I said in unison.

"How would you girls like to have yourselves a job?"

"With all due respect, Ms. Idella, no thanks. We love being volunteers, we don't want to get paid. What we do is from the heart," I replied sincerely.

"I know that, girls. I wasn't talking about working here. I own the new restaurant that's opening near the Beans."

"I heard about a restaurant opening near the Beans. They've been working on it for a couple weeks now. Dang, Mrs. Idella, you got the juice, boo," Shuntae said laughing

"Girls, I try, but really, I gave the restaurant to my grandson. He should be here in a few minutes. Matter a fact, there he is coming through door."

My eyes bucked when I saw Squeeze walk through the door. Who would have thought I would see this fine specimen again, but here he was.

"Hey, son, these are the young ladies I was talking about to hire for the restaurant. This is Palace and Shuntae, and I vouch for them. They are very good girls, Squeeze, and I know they will do great in the restaurant," Mrs. Idella said, holding our hands. "Squeeze, baby, you okay? You don't look well," Mrs. Idella said with a frown.

"Grandma, I'm fine. I just think I have a little bug. I mean, I been sick for a couple of weeks."

"Well child, let me get you out of here. You can't be making my people sick. Just gone, child, because I can't afford the people to get sick because of you."

Squeeze didn't look well at all, and I wanted to sex him back to health but I knew that was out the question. As Ms. Idella walked him out, I was watching him like a hawk.

"Palace, girl, is that the Squeeze you been with?" Shuntae pulled me in and whispered.

"Yes, that would be him, girl."

"Girl, I give it to you, Palace. That boys is fiiiiiinnnnnneee..."

Chapter 14

(Squeeze – Damn every time I try.)

My grandmother told me to come to the shelter because she had some new servers for the restaurant. I was really dragging my feet to get there. I had been sick for like three weeks now and I was weak as fuck. The only reason I hadn't called my doctor yet was because in the fall, I always caught a little common cold. This wasn't no common cold, though, and I didn't like it at all. It was cuddling season and I wasn't the dude that cuddled with chicks, but right now, I wished I had a girl.

I saw Palace in the shelter with my grandma and the night we'd shared came flooding back in my memory. It was unprotected sex but it was good. I really wanted to talk to her about the night we shared and get to know her a little more. I was hoping I would get that chance but that was short-lived when my grandmother told me to leave.

I got in my truck and headed straight to my house to get back in my bed. I wished my grandma would have made me some soup. I knew it was coming, maybe later, but I needed something now. I wondered if my mom would take care of me. I wondered if her motherly instincts would kick in, just for today, so I called her up.

"Hey, Ma, what you doing?"

"Squeeze, is that you?"

"Yeah, Ma, it's me."

"Boy, you sound bad. What's going on with you?"

"I don't know. I'm sick as a dog. I keep throwing up. I can't hold anything down and I want me some Skittles bad. I can't even eat them, they make me sick, too." Skittles were my favorite candy. I ate them like I drank water, which was a lot.

"Boy, you are a grown ass man. Get your ass up and go to CVS or Walgreens and fix whatever you got going on. My baby days are over except when my grandbabies come, and you know they don't stay but for an hour or two."

"Okay, Mom, I love you. Talk to you later."

I knew that hope would be short-lived but I'd tried. I got in my house and went straight to bed.

Chapter 15

(Princess – should I?)

I was loving my freshman year at FSU. It was good to see new faces even though I saw a few old ones, too. I was loving my dorm, Ty Hall, and my roommate Unique was off the chain. Who knew being away from home in the same state could be interesting?

Unique persuaded me to go out for a sorority. I was skeptical at first but after much consideration, I decided to do it. The rush week was starting soon and I was nervous. What was going to come out of this? I was going out for Alpha Kappa Alpha. It's a "Legacy of Sisterhood and Service." I had seen the Alphas around the campus, and I was scared that I would not be a match for the ladies. I would just have to wait to see if I could uphold a position in the sorority.

I was in the dining hall eating by my lonesome when I saw this fine man walking in. I mean, as soon as he hit door, women were all over him. I was staring at him so hard I didn't even hear Unique come sit at the table.

"Girl, everybody want some Zane," Unique said.

"Who is Zane?"

"Zane is the man you're drooling over right now."

"I can't help it. That man is some kind of sexy, Unique."

"Well, join the crowd then, Princess, because he has one."

I could not help but to stare at this man. His pearly white teeth, low cut fade, sexy ass chest, and brown skin had me mesmerized. I had to admit that there was some saliva forming in the cracks of mouth as I was lusting over this man.

"Princess, he is a straight up hoe. All he does is hit'em, and quit'em. He ain't worth your precious jewels down there."

"I hear you, girl," I told Unique. My phone started ringing and I answered without even looking at my caller ID.

"Hey, Princess, I miss you," I heard Palace sing.

"Little sis, I miss you, too. What's going at home? I haven't heard from you in hot minute."

"I got into it with Momma a couple weeks back, and I been working at a homeless shelter. Well, Shuntae and I have been working at a homeless shelter. I think we got ourselves a job at a restaurant that is opening near the Beans."

"Dang, Palace, at least you doing something outside of school. I'm proud of you and Shuntae. I always knew y'all had giving hearts. The situation with Mom, we will talk about later. How about you, Shuntae, and Pierre come spend the weekend up here with Prince and I? What is Pierre up to, anyway?"

"Pierre is good. You know him, he is doing his thing. I'm glad I can come see you because I need my hair done."

"Well, just call me and let me know when you want us to come pick you up. I love you, Palace. I got to get to class, I will talk to you later."

I hung up the phone with my sister and got ready for class. As Unique and I headed to the door, I looked at Zane one more time, only to see him cuddled with Jewella. All the lusting I had for that man went right out the door. I'd hated Jewella since she tripped me in the hallway in eighth grade. I fell flat on my face and I was teased for weeks about it and I hated her for that. She had a little crew she hung with called "the let's get it crew." She and her crew they thought they were better than everyone else. I didn't see it because she was from the Beans just like I was, so whatever.

As I got outside, I saw my brother Prince and Travis, his best friend.

"What's up, Bro?"

"What's up, Sis? And hey, Unique."

"Prince, I talked to Palace today and I thought it would okay if they came up here one weekend."

"That's cool with me. I've missed my little brother and sister, so yeah, that's what's up. I have a date with this girl name Carmen tonight," Prince grinned.

"What, my brother going on an actual date? That's what's up. I am proud of you! Where are you taking the young lady tonight?"

"Shit, you know a brother ain't got it like that so I'm taking her to Red Lobster."

"Okay, I see you, bro. I know you've never been to Red Lobster so I hope you enjoy yourself."

"Thanks! Love ya, Sis, see you later. Bye, Unique."

My brother gave us a hug and left. Unique and I headed to class so we could chill later on at a party.

Chapter 16

(Prince – Can't believe my eyes)

I was getting ready for my date with Carmen. I wasn't really into girls like that. I was focused on my good grades and football. My sister and I were the first ones in our family to ever go to college. I just wanted to make my granny proud. My granny was a straight hard body. She didn't play no games, but she meant well with everything she did. She had a spirit of an angel and the heart of a lion.

Princess didn't like the way our grandmother spoke to us. But the way she spoke to us and beat our tail was why we were in college today. If she didn't stay on us like she did, there's no telling what we could be in because our mother really didn't care. I respected my grandmother so much and I had to make her proud of me.

I looked at myself in the mirror and I had to say to myself, "Damn, that boy fine as hell."

I headed to Carmen's dorm to pick her up. As soon as I approached the door, Carmen came out smiling from ear to ear. I had to admit she was sexy as hell. Carmen Tadley was about 5'2, 120 pounds. Her measurements were perfect, 36-24-36. I couldn't deny her if I tried. She had me mesmerized with her big boobs and big hazel eyes. I couldn't figure why she'd decided to ask me for date but when she did, I had to make sure that Ashton Kutcher didn't jump out to prank my ass.

I wasn't ugly by any means but I just didn't get that much play in high school. Pierre and I were known for football because we were just that good. All the play I got was just because I was the quarterback. I would hit every now and then because I was a man that had needs from time to time. All the high school girls were just trying to get a name just to say that they were with the quarterback. I wasn't really feeling them and they never wanted to know the real me. I hoped Carmen wasn't like that. Besides, she was the first real date I ever had. The other girls got McDonalds.

We walked to my car and I opened the door for her to get in. The Gucci sweater dress was hugging her curves something serious. As soon as I got in and started the car, she started to spark up a conversation.

"I'm glad that you decided to on this date with me, Prince."

"How could I turn down a lovely lady as yourself? I was happy you asked me."

"I been checking you out for a while and I just could not take another day without saying a word to you."

I was starting to feel like she was just another groupie so I just had to give it her straight, no chaser. I was feeling shorty and I didn't want her to hurt my feelings because she wanted a come up. I had feelings like everyone else in this world so no I didn't want to take any chances.

"Carmen, if you're out with me because of my football status, we can turn right back around. I like you and all but it ain't worth me getting hurt in the end."

I saw the look on her face and I regretted saying that to her. It was like her whole face had dropped to the floor. I was in my zone. I didn't realized that we were almost at Red Lobster.

"I can understand where you are coming from, Prince. I would understand how you could think something like that. However, I can assure you that you playing football isn't what is most attractive in this case. I really want to know you the real you. I look at you in class and can tell that you have talent, and you are very good in science, might I add. There's more to you than football, and I can see that with flying colors."

My face had hit the floor. I never heard a girl admire me like she did. If other girls did say anything like that, all they knew was that I played football. Carmen looked at me outside of football and that was a plus in my book. I was praying that we would hit it off on another level, and not sex, either.

I parked my car and went to grab the door for Carmen to get out. As we were entering the restaurant, Carmen grabbed my hand. She was bold as hell and I liked it. As we waited for the hostess to take us to our seat, I noticed dimples in Carmen's smile. I thought they were so cute. She had one in each cheek and they enhanced her facial features, making her flawless. The hostess came back and led the way to our table. I pulled out her chair and we both looked at the menu. I was glad I'd brought over a hundred dollars because, shit, seafood was expensive as hell.

I thought that Red Lobster only did shrimp and fish. shit, that was the only seafood I knew about. I looked the menu and the prices were crazy but the food looked good as hell, I can't front. I thought about the choices I had and I was like fuck it, let me eat like a king for a day because I definitely had a queen before me. I ordered us shrimp nachos for our appetizer. As we were eating, we started to understand one another a little more. Before we knew it, the waitress came with our dinner entrees. Carmen had ordered the Admiral's Feast because she really could not decide what she wanted. I looked at the plate and would be in awe if this girl could eat all that was on her plate. Since I only knew shrimp and fish, I wanted something a little different so I settled for Bar Harbor Lobster Bake.

I had to admit that the food was by far the best the meal I'd ever had besides my grandmother's food. I was about to ask for the check when Carmen grabbed my hand and looked me in my eyes.

"Prince, I know this our first date and all, but I want to be much more than that."

"What you mean, like my girl or something?" I had to say it like that because I was caught off guard. I'd love for her to be my girl, and I could not deny the feeling she made me have.

"Well, you didn't have to say it like that. Sorry for even mentioning it."

"I'm sorry, Carmen. I was just caught off guard. Of course I would love for you to be my girl."

Chapter 17

(Princess-Party time)

I was ready to get my party on! Unique and I were getting ready to go make something shake. I wasn't feeling it at first but that quickly changed. I hadn't been out in a while and it might have been just what I needed to get me out the funk I was in. I had to remember that this was rush week and anything could happen at any given time. I learned that lesson when I watched the movie *Stomp The Yard*.

I took my shower and I went to my vanity to prep myself with my makeup, hair, lotion, and perfume. I was Michael Kors down from head to toe. I wore my red Michael Kors sweater with my black Michael Kors ripped jeans, and MK boots. I also had my MK purse and earrings, compliments of my booster Lourine. That girl could steal anything and that's why I depended on her for the best clothes that I could not afford. Unique had on some designer clothes that I could not even pronounce but she was fly has hell, though. I knew she had on some Louboutin heels that I knew set her back a pretty penny. I could not wait for the day that I could afford nice things like that but for now, I had to settle for what Lourine could get.

When I walked up the party, I saw fraternities showing their moves for the other team to compete. I was astonished by the moves they were giving each other. I loved stepping that's really what made me pledge in the beginning. Unique and I stepped through the party and we got stares from the girls and the guys wanted us on a platter. Rich Gang ft. Young Thug "Lifestyle" started to play and I was in the groove. I started singing to the beat.

I've done did a lot of shit just to live this here

Lifestyle

We came straight from the bottom, to the top,

My lifestyle

Nigga living life like a volcano and this only

Beginning

I'm on the top of the mountain puffin on clouds and niggas still beginning

Million five on a Visa card

Hundred bands still look like the fuckin tires

Nigga servin great white like I'm feedin sharks

I won't do nothing with the bitch, she can't even get me hard

Something wrong with the pussy

Even though I ain't gon hit it I'ma still make sure

That she gushy

Me and my woadie, we don't get caught up like

That, no way

We ain't time to go see doctors, J

(Who said money?)

Hop up in my bed full of forty bitches and yawning

Hey, this a show bitch you performing

I do this shit for my daughters and all my sons bitch

I'm a run up them band, I'll take out their funds

Bitch

I got a moms, she got a moms bitch

I got sisters and brothers to feed

I ain't going out like no idiot, I'm a OG

I was singing and rocking my hips until I felt a pair of hands wrap around my waist. I looked up. I didn't know who this guy was but he followed my lead so I just let him dance with me for the rest of the song.

When the song stopped, I turned to him. "Thanks for the dance," I told this handsome man standing in front of me.

"No, thank you. I'm Kareme, and you are?"

"Nice to meet you. My name is Princess." I was about to go and find Unique when he grabbed my hand.

"Can I get your number, Ms. Princess?"

I gave him a smile as he handed me his pen to write my number. This man was fine. He stood at least 6'3 and his body build was made only for a football player. His brown skin and long dreads had me in awe. As I was finished writing my last digit, Unique came out of nowhere.

"Hey, girl, this party is the bomb," Unique was slurring in her words so I knew it was time to go.

I grabbed Unique's hand and pulled her out the door to head to our dorm. She was saying some shit that I could not understand. I guess that was the liquor talking because I could have sworn that she was speaking Chinese. I looked at my drunk friend and said to myself, "It's going to be a long night."

Chapter 18

(Palace - Family weekend with surprises)

I had been anxiously waiting all week for Shuntae, Pierre, and I to spend the weekend with Prince and Princess. I called Princess an hour ago. She was finally outside, blowing the horn like she was too good for the Pork and Beans. I gave my grandma a kiss and we were out. I could not wait to get on campus to see how my sister and brother lived. I wanted the campus life so bad. I would watch reruns of *A Different World* just to enjoy the view of their college life. I was so glad that this was my last year of high school because I would to be out on my own in no time.

As soon my foot hit the cement on campus, my stomach felt queasy. I guess it was just my nerves messing with me because I'd been waiting for a taste of this lifestyle. I had been looking through some college pamphlets for the last three days. FSU was my first choice because my sister and brother were there but I would be lying if I said I would not want to go to A&T in Greensboro, NC. I had heard about GHOE for years and never got a chance to go. Gold and Blue. I could see myself rocking Aggie pride!

Snapping out my thoughts, I noticed a girl with long, pretty hair. She reminded me of Jennifer Lopez a little bit. She came straight to us, gave hugs, and when she spoke, I finally knew just who this high pitched diva was.

"Unique, is that you?" I knew it was her but I had to play the role.

"Yes, boo, it's me! The one and only," as she gave me another hug.

I saw Prince running up with a girl I didn't know, but didn't care. I was so happy to see my brother. He gave us hugs that were extra tight.

"Brah, who this pretty lady with you?" I quizzed.

"Palace, this my lady, and, if all goes well, your future sister-in-law, Carmen."

I didn't know much about Carmen but her presence felt loving and warm. I knew I would like her. Shuntae and I were staying with

Princess and Unique and Pierre was staying with Prince. We began walking to the dorm and I saw some fine dudes that I knew had to be blessed by Gods. Who knew Black men could be this flyy and sexy? In the Pork and Beans, the guys were sagging pants, dirty dreads, stinky breath, sell drugs, and hit every girl around. Prime example: Squeeze's sexy ass. That's why I could never see myself with him because of the image he portrayed. I knew that he had something to do with the new restaurant that was around the way, but all I saw is what I'd met. He was straight up thug, and a common one at that.

"Girl, what the hell do you want done to this nappy head of yours?" Princess screamed at me.

I didn't remember how I managed to get in her room or how I was sitting in a chair about to get my hair done. "Do I have to get my hair done now? Can't we wait till we scan the campus?" I asked Princess.

"Hell no, Palace. Before we get our day started, my sister has to be looking flyy walking through here. If you want to catch you a good one, you want to be flyy. First impressions are the best impressions. These brothers around here are on their Ps and Qs, boo. On that note, please reach over there and hand me that pack of hair. I'm going to hook you up because we're going out tonight, college style."

I never been to a club a day in my life. I was game for this adventure. I reached over to grab the hair off the bed and I felt something warm. As I leaned back I looked at my shirt and it had two wet spots.

"Palace, what the fuck is that?"

"I don't know. it's like my boobs are leaking or something. This has never happened before."

My sister, Unique, and Shuntae had their hands over their mouths looking at me like they were crazy.

"What? Why y'all looking at me like that?"

"Palace, you are pregnant if your boobs leaking like that." Princess had tears in her eyes.

This had to be some kind of mistake. I could not be pregnant right now. I could not be pregnant, period! This had to be some kind of joke or something. How? No, why? Not me, not my life! No!

"Palace, how this happen? I thought that you were a virgin," my sister said, crying and yelling at me.

IRISH LAHCHYNA

Before I knew it, everything went black.

Chapter 19

(Squeeze - Can't get her out of my mind)

I was feeling better than ever. My grandma seemed to nurse me back to health with her soup and home remedies. I was still nauseous sometimes but it eased off a lot thanks to my grandma. I had some good days and some bad ones. I went to Doctor Anderson and he could not find a thing wrong with me. He chopped it up to a bug going around and said that it would pass. But he didn't tell me it would take almost two months to pass.

I hadn't seen Palace in a while and I couldn't get her off my mind. It was like she was avoiding me or something. I would go by the new shelter that Grandma built on the Southside. When I got there, she would be gone or she wasn't coming in that day. I just wanted to talk to her to see where her head was at. Every time I would ask Pierre, he would just stick to our business arrangement we had, that was it. But I knew something was off about the whole thing. I could feel it. I wasn't going to sweat at this point because I had a business meeting to attend to.

I wanted to make sure that everyone has a place to live and that was my next project I was working on. I had a meeting with the mayor about buying some land to build a housing complex for the homeless and help them get on their feet. My heart could not stand the fact that there were people out living on the streets. It wasn't right and the economy didn't make it any better. It was hard to live in this world. I just wanted to make it easier for some people. I was happy that the mayor granted me permission to start on my project. When I went into his office, I could see the stares of people because of my appearance but if they only knew what qualities I possessed. Looks can be deceiving. When will people ever learn that?

Chapter 20

(Paris - It was now or never)

I'd just copped me a gram of that good stuff from Lil' Pete. I swear that dude know how to give what I needed. I was feeling lovely. I was unstoppable and prettier than any female out here. Shit, I got the juice. Shit, the men wanted me to be their queen. I was headed to interview for a job. I was about to get my family back and I would do everything in my power to do it. I had just gotten my hair done. My nails were on fleek and my makeup was flawless. I had on my Gucci outfit that I'd stolen from Palace's room so I knew I was fly as hell.

I was strutting my stuff and lo and behold, I see my husband, once again with this woman that he'd left his family for. I was going to get my man back today. Shit, look at me! Who would not want me? I was a flyy ass woman that had it all. It was time that I made my presence known and let this woman know that my husband belonged to me.

I walked into the restaurant where Prince Sr. and this woman were sitting. I walked straight up to the table.

"So this the heffa you left your family for? Look at me now, Prince. I manage to still look better than this tramp you prancing around town with. How could you just leave us like that, huh? I gave you my heart and you left on your fucking son's birthday! His first birthday, at that. What kind of man would do that shit to his family, huh? Now you get the fuck up because you coming back home where you belong."

I stood there with my hands on my hips and turned to the woman who had to be mixed. He was fucking with funky compared to me. I was a diamond. She just knew I was flyy as shit right now.

"What the fuck, Paris? Look at yourself! Ain't no way I would stoop as low to go back to your ass. Look at yourself. You are disgusting, and you smell! How could I even want you in the state you are in? And you question why I left? You actually want to question me about why I left your ass?! I never wanted to leave my kids but if I didn't, I would be looking like you right about now." Prince Sr. looked at me with his nose up and grabbed his wife's hand and left the restaurant.

My high went all the way down as I looked at the reflection of myself in the window. The once flyy hairdo I had was now hair sticking up on top of my head. The Gucci outfit I had on was ripped, dirty, and had a stench of old coochie and piss. My nail paint was now chipped, just nail polish with speckles of dirt. My makeup was patches of dirt and some bruises that I'd gotten while fighting for my stem.

I looked at myself and I was ashamed of what I looked like. Crack can make you feel so good but you're so dirty inside and out. I continued to stare at my reflection with tears in my eyes as the manager came in yelling at me to get out of his restaurant. I was scaring his customers away. I had just made a complete fool of myself in front of Prince Sr. and his lady. I got to get myself together for my family.

But on the other hand, that was some good shit to make feel like that. I should go get me another hit before I get myself together. I didn't know. I wanted to feel good and make all this hurt go away. Then again, I could just go to rehab to compress the pain and change for the better.

"Hey, Paris, you want hit this shit with me? I got this from Lil' D Rock across the way. You know he got that good shit." My girl Carla was pulling me by my shirt going in the alley to take a hit.

I guess I would do rehab tomorrow.

Chapter 21

(Palace – Nah, this can't be happing to me)

I woke up the next day in the hospital with Shuntae, Princess, and Unique at my bedside.

"We must have partied up something last night because I had the weirdest dream. What did I do? Did I pass out from drinking so much? That's why I'm in the hospital, right, Princess?"

My sister just looked at me and shook her head. "Palace, tell us about the dream you had because we would all like to hear this, my lovely little sister," Princess finally responded.

"It was a dream that we were all in the dorm and my boobs started to leak and y'all told me I was pregnant. Isn't that crazy, Princess?"

"No, that ain't crazy. In fact, Palace, it's the truth. Now what I want to know is why now, Palace? You just messed up your whole life up! Who is the father, girl?"

"This can't be real right now," I was still in disbelief.

The doctor came in while I was looking stupid. "Hello ladies, how's the patient today? I see you are up, Ms. Slain."

"Hello, Doctor–"

"I'm Doctor Langston, Palace. I'm sorry, do you mind if I call you Palace?"

"No, I don't mind at all. Can you please tell me what's going on, Dr. Langston?"

"First of all, would you like for your friends to stay or should we talk in private?"

"They can stay, doctor. It's fine with me.

"Well, Palace, you are seven weeks pregnant."

I looked at the doctor like he had grown two heads because I knew there was no way that I could be pregnant. Not now. A baby wasn't in my plans at all. I had a future after graduating this year. I was going to school to become a doctor! A baby would only complicate things for me. I could not have this baby and on top that, the father was a thug! I could not chance this.

I started crying as Doctor Langston left room to give me alone time with my girls.

"Palace, what in the world were you thinking? Girl, Grandma is going to have a fit when she finds out. On top of that, Prince, Pierre, and Mom."

"Well, they ain't going to find out because I can't have this baby. The daddy is just another statistic in the neighborhood. Nah, I will not have my baby around the drug nor hood life. I'm just going to get abortion tomorrow." I looked at Princess, Unique, and Shuntae.

"Oh, the hell if you are! We don't believe in abortions in this family. Palace, you are going to deal with this and finish school. The daddy we will work on, but we are all here for you no matter what. Who is the daddy anyway, again I ask."

I was trying so hard to avoid answering that question from my sister but I knew it would come out soon or later anyway. "My baby's daddy is Squeeze."

"Squeeze! The Squeeze that I hear about in the streets? The man is paid from what I hear in the streets. So, how did this happen, you meeting him? Wait a minute. Palace, you had unprotected sex with this man and he the man in the streets? I know he been with lots of girls. You could have caught anything from his ass."

I was on the verge of telling my sister off when the nurse came in with my discharge papers and my prescription for prenatal vitamins.

"Okay, Palace, I know you're mad at me but I have to ask you this. You haven't had any symptoms?"

"No, I didn't, but I know Squeeze has been sick lately."

"Girl, you're lucky. He got the morning sickness and you didn't. He might have all the symptoms and don't have a clue to what's going on."

We all started laughing while I was getting dressed to go back to the campus with my sister.

Chapter 22

(Squeeze - Hood life)

"Roll the muthafuckin dice, nigga," I told the nigga with the dice. I loved taking niggas' money on the block. I really didn't need it I just like taking the money from these old heads around here.

"Squeeze, man, you always trying to hustle us, man," some dude said to me.

"Nah, man. Y'all asses just don't know how to fuckin shoot dice," I replied.

I felt my phone vibrating. I saw it was the girl that I thought would be my forever love. I liked Megan a lot in high school but when I overheard the conversation that she had with some of her homegirls, it hurt me to my heart.

"*Megan, girl how long you been with Squeeze?*"

"*Kenyatta, I been with Squeeze for three months now.*"

"*It seems like your ass is in love, Megan. I mean Squeeze is a nice ass dude.*"

"*In love? Girl, who said I was in love with Squeeze? I ain't in love with him. I'm in love with his pockets. Kenyatta, girl, I got me a college dude that tap this ass very nice. My dude is good to me but his pockets ain't like Squeeze's, though.*"

"*Megan, girl, that shit ain't right to use that boy like that.*"

"*What he don't know won't hurt him.*"

Well, that shit did hurt like hell. I was really feeling her, too. The next day when I went to school, I ignored her ass and I cut her ass off. After that, my heart was cold toward all the girls. She'd made it bad for anyone who wanted a chance with me.

That's why I couldn't have a main girl, because my heart was messed up by one. I couldn't front, though. Palace had a nigga feeling some kind of way. That night had me all in my feelings about her and wanted to talk to her in the worst way. My heart was scared of commitment, though.

I took those old coons' money and hopped in my truck. I was heading home to make a pit stop before going to hit Megan off. Soon as I got out my truck good, I heard my name being called.

"Deontae, Deontae."

I heard my next door neighbor, Ms. Paulina call me. She was the only one that called me by government name. My full name was Deontae Bytiness.

"Yes ma'am, Ms. Paulina?"

"Oh, I'm Ms. Paulina now? I used to be Momma Paulina. Are you losing love for the old lady?" She smiled at me but she was right. I'd always called her Momma Paulina. I didn't why I said that. it just came out that way.

"No Ma'am. It came out wrong."

"Can you pull my trash can to the road? And tell Ms. Idella I have some clothes for the shelter."

"Yes ma'am, no problem."

After I pulled the trash, I went in my house, grabbed my condoms, then headed out to give Megan some of my wood and dip out.

Chapter 23

(Palace - Here go nothing)

I'd had to a lot to take in and consider since I found out that I was carrying a baby. I couldn't process that fact that in about seven months I would be someone's mother. One night of being mad at my mother caused all this. It sure was a blessing and curse at the same time. I hadn't told my brothers yet. Next to know was my grandmother. I took a deep breath as I got out of my sister's car to head in the house to face my grandmother.

"Girl, are you good? Do you need me to be in there with you?" Shuntae asked me as we stood in front of my grandmother's door.

"Nah, I'm good. I think I need to handle this alone." I gave Shuntae a hug and she went into her house.

Pierre was in and out in a rush. He was in a hurry to Peanut's house. He couldn't wait to tell Peanut about all the thick girls and the phone numbers he'd gotten. I walked in and my granny was sitting in her recliner watching *Wheel of Fortune*.

"Hey, Palace, how was your weekend with your brother and sister?"

"It was good, Grandma."

"I can't tell with the look on your face. What's wrong, is something bothering you? Did something happen while you were gone, girl?"

I put down my bags and sat down on the couch to prepare myself to tell my grandmother what the deal was. "Grandma, there is something that I need to tell you."

"Lord, child, quit taking your time and tell me what's wrong."

"Grandma, I'm pregnant."

"I knew it. I dreamt of fish the other night."

I thought my grandma was going to pull out the belt on me. I had never been so scared in my life. "Fish?" I asked her before I heard the front door slam.

"Palace, you're pregnant, girl?"

My mom came in the door like a mad woman, a stinky one at that. I looked at my mom and she had on my Gucci outfit that I'd gotten from Brooke. It was well worn, dingy, and dirty. The only reason I knew it was mine because the collar and a little ink mark from an accident with my favorite pen. This was not the way I wanted her to find out, but it is what it is. My grandmother looked at me and put her finger to her lips, hushing me. We would talk later, without my mom ear hustling. I got up from the couch and looked at my mother with disgust in my eyes.

"Palace, are you pregnant? And this the last time I'm going to ask you this."

"Why do you care? It's not like you would be around to help me. Look at yourself! You can't even pick up a brush or keep your hygiene in order, but you want to question me about my life. For your information, yes, I'm pregnant. As if that is any of your business."

I could not look at my mother like that. I could not understand why she had her life hanging by a thread with drugs. I understood why my father left years ago and she should have gotten over it by now. My mom was so pretty. Any man would have her if she would get her life together but I guess that's not what she wanted.

Chapter 24

(Shuntae – Friends is what they call them)

I walked in my house with a lot on the brain. My best friend was about to be a mother and I couldn't be happier. I was happy that I was going to be an auntie soon. I was going to be there for Palace in any way that I could because in the months ahead, I knew she was going to need it. Palace wanted to get an abortion and I was glad that Princess deaded that shit because there wasn't any way I could let my best friend do that. I knew that she didn't want to be finishing high school with a belly but GOD did that for reason. It ain't no telling what good could come out of this.

I walked in my room and I looked on my bed and there was a hundred dollars laying on my pillow. I knew it was from my brother Danger because he always did things like that. I loved my brother dearly and was very grateful that he gave me money every now and then. On the flip side of that, I wanted a relationship with someone that could provide for me as well.

After we left the hospital and got back to the campus, we ended up going to a club on the East end. It was Palace's and my first time going to a club. I must say we enjoyed ourselves. I met this guy name Shyheim, Sy, for short. He wasn't from Florida at all, he was from New York and he was visiting family. He stood 5'7, had light skin, blue eyes, was heavily tatted, and had long dreads. That was the kind of man I needed. He wasn't from here and didn't know a thing about my brother. All I ever wanted was a real relationship and hopefully I could get one with Sy.

I picked up my phone and decided to call Brooke and Nicole to tell them what was going on with Palace. We'd been friends like forever and we all had each other back. Palace needed all the help she could get and we needed to be her support system.

"Hey, Brooke, what's up with you, boo?"

"Nothing, girl. Me and Nicole chilling at the crib doing nothing. Girl, Peanut had a nerve to leave my ass at Chris's party. I ain't even mad, though. I got his ass, girl."

"Girl, I don't know what to say about you and Peanut. But anyway, put Nicole on speaker phone. I need to talk to y'all about something."

"Okay, we are on speaker. Go ahead, Shuntae, what's up?" Brooke yelled in the phone so loudly I had to put my phone on speaker.

"Look, y'all, we need to be there for Palace in the best way right now. She is going to need us now more than ever."

"Why, Shuntae, what's going on with Palace?" Nicole asked

"Palace is pregnant and we all are going to be aunties."

I heard them yelling and screaming all in my ear. I knew they were going to be happy. Brooke had a thing for babies.

"Oh my gawd, I'm so happy. I'm going to be there for her every step of the way. What if she has twins?" Brooke was past excited.

I didn't get the same feeling from Nicole, though. It was like something was on her mind. She wasn't as happy as I thought she would be.

"Nicole, what's up with you?" I asked

"Nothing, I'm happy for Palace. I have one question, though. Who is the baby's daddy?"

"I will let her tell you both that. It wasn't really my place to tell y'all she is pregnant but because we are best friends, I just wanted to give y'all the heads up. I'm getting ready to go to bed. I will see y'all at school tomorrow. Love y'all guys."

I hung up the phone and headed to the bathroom to take my shower and then to bed.

Chapter 25

(Nicole – Friend or foe??)

Who would have thought that Ms. Goody Two Shoes Palace would get knocked up? I loved Palace, we'd been friends for years. She and I were best friends first. Before Shuntae and Brooke came along, it was always me and her. When you saw me, you saw her, and that was the way we rocked until Shuntae became her bestie. It was like she put our friendship on the back burner when Shuntae came in the picture.

Before Palace even moved to the Pork and Beans Projects, I knew her. We were both living in Atlanta, Georgia, going to the elementary school together. Our mothers were something like best friends but I wouldn't say the best of friends. Ms. Paris and my mother, Athena, would fuss like cat and dogs one day then be friends the next. It was something that I could not understand to save my life. Palace's family was going through some issues and before I knew it, my best friend was moving away from me. I never really knew what part of Florida she was moving to. I just knew she was moving. My mother got sick a couple of years later with breast cancer and couldn't take care of the responsibilities anymore. My mother, brother, Tyshawn, and I were evicted from our home and were forced to come live with my auntie in the suburbs in Florida.

When my brother and I started school here, we hated it. Auntie didn't want us to go to public school so she put us in a Christian private school. When we got to middle school, my mother kicked cancer's butt and was healthy once again. My mother got a job and purchased a house five miles outside the Pork and Beans Projects. My mom knew that me nor my brother liked private school so she put us in public schools. That's when Palace and I reconnected but it wasn't the same as before.

I'd missed our friendship something terrible and that was partly why I cut up at the private school. I was low-key hoping that I would be kicked out and forced to go to public school. I was hoping if that happened, I would hopefully run into Palace. We were all friends but I couldn't stand the relationship that Palace and Shuntae shared. Palace hurt me and I wanted her to know how I felt in the inside.

I knew that Palace had slept with Squeeze. That's why I was going to make sure that he was in my bed soon. I was hoping that he was her baby daddy because it would make my plan a little better. I wanted to make her hurt like she'd hurt me.

Chapter 26

(Paris - Maybe a second chance)

I was sitting up in the crack house on Ashe Street looking at all the addicts that were around me. I wasn't sure what came over me but I didn't feel like getting high today. Little Pete and Slow Fire were giving me free dope all day but I couldn't strike my lighter to take a hit. It had been four days since I'd rushed in mother's house to play the role of distressed child. I'd told mother that someone was out to get me. I acted it out so well that I should have won an Academy Award, a Grammy or something. That was the only for sure way that my mother would give me money freely and willingly. I didn't know that I would come through the door to find out that my baby girl was about to make me a grandmother.

I got up and looked at my homeboy, Fletcher, who always shared his pipe with me.

"Fletch, I'm out of here. I can't do this no more. it ain't in me."

He looked at me and smiled. I was about to walk away before he grabbed my hand to help him up off the nasty, pissy mattress we were sitting on.

"Sweet Paris, if this ain't for you, then ain't for me, neither."

I looked at this man that been in every crack house I had been and turned more tricks than I could count just to get high. His face was stone cold and dirty. His once caramel complexion was ashy white and his teeth were tarnished brown and yellow. I couldn't read his expression but the way he was holding my hand, I knew he was walking out the door with me.

We walked out the door hand in hand as we were headed to the rehabilitation center to start our lives over.

Chapter 27

(Squeeze – Say what!!!)

It was the weekend so I knew I could catch Palace at the shelter if I got there early enough. I woke up mad early. I had to make sure that the restaurant was ready to open up next week. I had handle my hygiene so I could be ready for today. I threw on my red, white, and blue Polo shirt, my Polo jeans, and my all white Air Force Ones. I hopped in my truck and headed straight to the shelter.

When I got to the shelter, I saw my mom hanging out on the sidewalk talking to a thug named Mack. I hated thugs. they was the prime example of what our Black community shouldn't stand for. I'd made my living by helping others and it wasn't a hard task by far. It was something I loved to do and I would not trade it for the world. I couldn't say the same about my mom, though. She was raised with the same values that my grandmother had shown me and my brothers. I didn't why but for some reason, my mom didn't get the memo.

"Yo, Ma, why you over there leaning in that car like you some teenager or something?"

"Squeeze, mind your own and leave me alone. I'm your momma, remember? You are not my daddy."

"I know that! That's exactly why you should not be bent over like that because you are a mother, not a child or a hooker."

I threw her another dirty look and shook my head as I entered the shelter. I was glad when I entered I saw my grandmother occupied with Ms. Cassie. Granny and Ms. Cassie had been best friends forever. They don't make friendships like there anymore. That's why I cherished what they had together. Their friendship was genuine and straight from the heart.

"Hey, Grandma and hey, Granny Cassie. What y'all doing over here?"

"Hey, baby, we are making preserves for the shelter," my grandmother said, giving my forehead a kiss.

IRISH LAHCHYNA

"Well, it looks good and I know it's good if y'all two have anything to do with it."

"Squeeze, I need for you make sure those young ladies get their uniforms for the restaurant and learn the ins and outs. I want it to be a success, baby. That's all."

"I got you, Grandma, and I understand. I'm about to head over to them now and talk with them. I will see you later." I gave my grandmother and Granny Cassie a kiss on the jaw before heading over to Palace and her friend Shuntae. "Hey, ladies, how are y'all doing today? I need to discuss the positions in the restaurant with you all."

"Okay, that's what's up. Let me know when and where, Mr. Squeeze, and I'm there. I need to go see what my little friend Markia is doing. I swear, if I ever have any children, I want my little girl to be just like her. I will be right back," Shuntae rambled on.

I looked at Palace and I could tell that something was wrong with her. She couldn't look at me, so I knew something wasn't right I felt it.

"Squeeze, can we please go somewhere to talk privately, please?" Palace asked me with her head still down and her eyes still staring at the floor.

"Sure, if you don't mind, we can go sit in my truck and talk." I led the way and she followed behind me outside to my truck. Once we got inside, I could tell that she'd gotten tense all of a sudden.

"What's up, Palace? You want to talk but now you're not saying anything."

"Squeeze, I don't know any other way to say this but I got to tell you. I'm pregnant."

I looked at her and shook my head. "Damn, Ma, what in the world! I don't why you felt the need to confide in me but I'm glad you did because I was feeling you."

She turned around with tears in her eyes and looked at me.

"Feeling me? Feeling me? that's all you can say. I confided in you because this is your baby just as well as mine. I knew it was mistake to tell you. I don't want you or your drug money. Just stay as far away from me and mine."

She hopped out my car and slammed my door. I was in complete shock and disappointed in myself. Truth be told, I wasn't anywhere near mentally ready to become someone's father. I didn't know what to do. My head was all the messed up.

Chapter 28

(Sarafenia – I'm grown)

I saw my son in the car with some girl. It looked like they were having a heated conversation but that wasn't any of my business. I was talking to Mack. I'd been dealing with Mack for years now and I was his girl. He was letting it be known around town that I wasn't to be fucked with. At first, I was okay with it because I loved me a thug. There was something about a man that rocked white tees, Timberlands, gold fronts, and had a pocket full of money. The fact that he sold drugs sparked a flame in me. I didn't know if was the thrill of the game or the respect that came with it that drew my attention but I liked it.

When I was first noticed as Mack's girl, I got mad respect but being his girl was messing up my money flow. I would be on stage at the club doing the routines that made me the most money and I wasn't pulling in shit. I had a fire routine where I put fire in my mouth and I licked that flame and put it between my pussy lips. That number always got me at least two thousand dollars but lately, I wasn't even making five hundred dollars. I wasn't having that so I was talking to Mack to tell him the deal.

"Hey, baby, what you doing around the way? I thought you had to attend some business today?" I quizzed

"I did, and I handled that already. I just was riding through to see my baby girl. Why don't you hop in for a minute? I see that big head son of yours think he got some hair on his balls talking to you like that." Mack's continued talking, showing his grill as I was getting in his car. There wasn't anything low-class about Mack, he liked the best of the best. He wasn't afraid to get robbed, either. People around this part knew he was not to be fucked with so he never got tried.

"Mack, baby, we need to talk."

"I'm listening, sweet cakes. What's on your mind?"

"Well, baby, I can't get no money in the club like I used to because I'm your girl."

"So, what's the fucking problem? I don't want your ass working there anyway. I told you I got you, baby."

I could see that Mack was getting upset.

"See, that's where you are wrong. I'm grown and I take care of me. I love you and your money but I'm self-sufficient all day. I just want you to please tone it down a little bit because I need that money."

Before I knew what was happening, Mack had grabbed me by the back of my neck. "Listen, you belong to me, bitch, and what I say goes. I want you to quit that fucking job. I got you, like I said. You're right, you may be grown, but I'm you motherfucking daddy!"

In all my years, I had never let a man put his hands on me and Mack wasn't going to be an exception. I reached into my pocketbook and pulled out my blade and put it under his chin.

"You might be the man in these streets and I don't what kind of bitches you fuck with. I'm telling you, playboy... get your fucking hands off me! And that's the last time you will put your dick beaters on me again."

I was scared shitless because I knew that this man was very powerful. I also knew if you give a man an inch, they will take a mile. That mile was something that I wasn't trying to see. Mack removed his hand from my neck while I still had my blade to his throat. I slowly pulled the door handle to get out his car. Once I was out his car, I got the hell out of Dodge. I ran to the other side of the building. I didn't know if he was going to follow me or not but I wasn't trying to see, either. Luckily, my car was on this side. I ran into my car and was out. I heard him scream while I was running away.

"This ain't over, Nia!"

And I knew that he wasn't lying.

Chapter 29

(Prince Sr. – Feeling is feelings)

I'd made the choice to leave my family a long time ago. Paris and I were fighting all the time and I couldn't take it anymore. One day we got invited to a friend's get together. We really needed the time to enjoy ourselves because between work and kids, we didn't really have that time. I worked at IBM and Paris worked as a secretary at a law firm. We were making good money and we were living well in Georgia. Our family was good and we lived comfortably until the night of that party.

We went to the party and it was very nice. Tammy and Marlon both worked with Paris at the law firm. They were successful lawyers in Georgia and friends of Paris and mine. The party was in full swing and we all were enjoying themselves. We started playing Spades and that's when another friend of ours, Carl, started passing around a joint. Everybody was passing, smoking, and carrying on like a party was supposed to be. We took a couple of pulls and realized this wasn't any ordinary weed we were smoking. It had us higher than we had ever been in our lives. It was good! It had us feeling like nothing could stop us. Plus it made us hornier than ever.

When we got home, we made love like we were dogs in heat. We loved the energy that drug gave us. The next day, the high came down and we rested up. But all we could think about was the high that we'd had last night and wanted it again. We called Tammy and Marlon to ask what was in the joint that we smoked. They told us it was a mixture of weed, crack, and ecstasy. Once we found out the ingredients to our new high, we were on it. Every day, we were getting high between jobs, at home, and even on our ten minute lunch breaks. We were getting high all the time. We could handle it for the most part, until we decided to try crack by itself. That's when things got out of hand.

It started to affect how we behaved at our jobs, then our bank accounts dwindled, and then our family suffered. We were constantly fussing about how the bills were piling up. I had turned into a full-time junkie and had almost quit my job. The relationship that Paris and I once had was now an abusive one. We started to physically fight each other over who would get the last hit of the pipe. I was tired of all the abuse. That fact it was affecting our children was too much to bear. Paris was pregnant with Pierre and getting high. I always prayed that he would turn out well. The Lord answered my prayers when he came out just fine. And the fact that he wasn't taken away from us was a bonus.

Pierre's first birthday was supposed to be a drug free day for us. We were supposed to be working on getting better for the sake of the kids. The kids were having a good time and our guests were as well. Before the cake was to be presented, Paris asked me to come in the room. I did what she asked me to and went inside the room.

"Prince, do have twenty dollars on you?"

"No. Paris, why do you need twenty dollars?"

"I need a quick fix real quick. Just so I can make it through this party."

"Nah, I'm not doing that. This is supposed to be Pierre's day and we said we would try to stop smoking."

Before I knew it, Paris had pulled out her gun on me. "I love you, Prince, and I never thought I would be doing this. I need you to go get me a twenty rock now! Before I have a nervous breakdown."

I was shocked and more scared than anything. I didn't want her to make a scene with all the kids there. I could not risk that. I backed up to the door and told her I was going to get her what she needed. I had made up my mind that I wasn't going back there. I closed our bedroom door. I went into the backyard and asked kids to come to me. I told the kids that I loved them and kissed their foreheads. I walked out that door and went straight to a rehabilitation center where I stayed for six months. I knew I was wrong for leaving my kids but if I went back, there was no telling what may have happened in that house. When I did come back after my treatment to see my children and get a divorce, Paris had up and moved away.

It wasn't until the other day when I saw Paris that I knew that I did the right thing by leaving. I never knew where she went. But now that I do, I wanted to find out where my kids were. I looked up her mother's name in the phonebook. I finally had the nerve to talk to the woman that hated my guts for years. After having a very brief conversation with her, she agreed to meet with me in three weeks. I didn't know why so long but I was just glad that she had agreed to meet with me at all.

Chapter 30

(Peanut – A struggle is a struggle)

I couldn't count on both of my hands how times I had cheated on Brooke. I loved her but it wasn't how it used to be. In ninth grade, I knew Brooke was the girl for me. She was the sweetest girl I'd ever known. The fact that she was pure, I mean never been touched, made me love her more. I never pressured Brooke to give me any because our relationship was just that good. We enjoyed each other's company and I knew that she wanted to be a virgin until she got married.

In tenth grade, Brooke wanted to start talking about sex and I always brushed the thought to the side. One day, we was at her house doing the usual, watching movies and cuddling up. We were watching *No Good Deed*. Brooke took our kissing and touching to a new level. She took my manhood out of my basketball shorts and went to work slurping me like it was a lollipop. I had been wanting that for so long that I didn't even stop her because it was feeling so good. She was doing it so good, and I had been faithful for two years. So yes, I was very backed up, all the way to ancient times, it seemed like. She did this little tongue action around head of my shaft while still slurping that had my head gone. She had me curling up my toes and before I knew it, I had exploded in her mouth. To my surprise, she swallowed and got up to straddle me. I was at full attention and she guided herself on top of me slowly. I didn't know where this was coming from but I was loving every minute of it.

Brooke was hurting. I could tell by the way she was tensing up but that did not make her stop doing what she was doing. Once she got the hang of me inside her, she was riding me like a stallion. I felt my nut building up once again, waiting to be released. I let her do a little more bouncing before I grabbed her by her waist and lifted her off me as my nut ran out. I was not planning on being a father soon so I had to make sure none of my seeds were up in her. That night changed the whole dynamic of our relationship.

The whole ordeal transformed Brooke in my eyes. She was not the shy little thing that I knew. She started to dress crazy, revealing more than skin than ever. She began to flirt with boys at our school more openly. That shit pissed me off but I knew that she wasn't going anywhere, so I just let that shit pass. That night also caused Brooke to be clingy to me, which made me more aggravated than ever. At that point, she wanted her cake and to eat it to. She wanted to be able to flirt and lead other guys on but wanted me to be up under her twenty-four, seven. She even got to the point of her accusing me of sleeping with every girl, when in fact, I was being faithful to her.

At the end of the day, I was still a man. She kept accusing me of messing around so I did it, on prom night. I wasn't really getting any from Brooke because she was busy trying to get other guys' attention. It was like she enjoyed what she was doing even though she had me. I felt neglected so I had sex with ole girl on prom night.

After cheating on her, we talked about it and got back together. I knew that it would not be the same but I didn't think it would be anything like it was now. Brooke played a role in front of her friends like I was always the bad one in our relationship when we both had played parts in the relationship going wrong. Brooke tried to come on to my best friend Pierre. There are some lines that you can't cross, and that was one of them.

When she would fuck up, I would just go out and cheat. This time was different, though. I been kicking it with Monique for three months now and she was pregnant with my seed. I felt it was time for me and Brooke to cut ties, we were about to graduate. I didn't know how I was going to break this to her but it had to be done sooner than later.

Chapter 31

(Brooke – Fighting for Love)

We were about three months from walking across the stage. I couldn't wait because I was tired of going to school. Twelve years of school was enough for me. I didn't really see what the rush was in going to college. I was going but in my time, not anyone else's. Shit, I needed some me time and I need to learn myself for once in my life.

I walked in school with my mind set on fighting this bitch named Monique. I'd been hearing that Peanut had been messing with her behind my back. This crow looking bitch knew that he was my man, and the fact that she continued to try and sleep with him had me heated. I didn't play when it came to Peanut.

True, we had our up and downs, but what relationship was perfect? Both of us were at fault when it came to our relationship issues. I had a good girl image to maintain. There was no way that I was going to let my girls know the real dirt that was going in in my relationship with Peanut.

Peanut was my first everything. He was my first love, first kiss, and my first sex partner. I couldn't let him go like that. I knew we were meant for each other and I wasn't going to let anyone come between us. Peanut was the only man that I had ever had sex with but if I had to be honest, I had a lustful mind. I would often wonder what other guys were like in bed and what the comparison would be to Peanut. When Peanut popped my cherry, it had my mind racing and my eyes began to lust. My mind got the best of me for sure with all my flirting. I didn't think it would backfire on me but it did. That was one of the reasons our relationship was where it was now. I had to keep a close eye on Peanut because I was scared of losing him.

I saw Monique going into the cafeteria alone so I felt that it was the time to confront this bitch and knock her ass out. I didn't know where my girls were but I knew they were nearby. She was by herself so it was only right that I was by myself also.

"Monique, what this I hear about you messing with Peanut?"

"Look, Brooke, not today because I don't feel like getting in it with you right now." She tried to walk past me but I wasn't trying to let her

"Whatever, bitch. I ain't going nowhere till you tell me what's the fuck is the shit that I keep hearing in the streets about you and my man."

"First of all, I ain't your bitch, and second of all, I don't have to explain a thing to you. That is Peanut's job. He is your man, so you say, right? Third, I'm a grown ass woman and I don't do all this yelling shit. If you want to talk, I will do that. But all this yelling shit is for the birds. I see you like attention, right, because you done grew a crowd of onlookers. That's not my style, shorty, so bye, Felicia."

I guess she called herself trying to check me but she was about to get served. She was trying to walk off again but this time, I grabbed her by her hair and I started tagging her head. I heard Peanut in the background screaming and then I heard my girls. Somebody was pulling me off of her but it wasn't Peanut. It was my girls pulling me off of Monique. When I looked up to see where Peanut was, he was crouching down helping Monique up like they were together or something.

I ran over to them.

"Peanut, what the fuck are you doing?"

"What the fuck does it look like I'm doing, Brooke? I'm helping her up!"

He kept helping her like I wasn't there or something. I was sitting here fighting for love and my love wasn't paying me no mind.

"Peanut, I was trying to be nice and act civil in this whole situation. But I can't sit back and let her keep coming at me sideways. You need to tell her what's up or I will," Monique was yelling at Peanut.

"What the hell is she talking about, Peanut?" I looked at him and he could not even look me in my eyes.

"I need to speak with you outside, Brooke, and please don't make a scene. It's bad enough you caused a crowd. Thankfully the teachers haven't come in yet."

I knew all too well the look he gave me. He wasn't playing any games. I just turned around and went outside so we could talk away from the listening ears that were around.

"What's up, Peanut? And this better be good. I'm tired of hearing you messing around on me. It's embarrassing and disrespectful as hell."

"Brooke, why you always playing the blame game like I'm so bad when you do just as much, if not more, than I do? Like the fact that you came on to my best friend! Did you think that he wasn't going to tell me? There are some lines that you should never cross and that's one of them. I would never come on to any one of your girls. I would not dare. The fact that you would even go that low told me a lot about you. What you heard about me and Monique is true. We have been messing around for three months now, and she is pregnant with my baby."

I looked at Peanut and all I saw was red. I wanted to rip his eyes out. I wanted to kill him right where he was standing but I kept my composure. I wasn't going to make a scene. Plus, maybe it was time for us to part ways. I was tired of fighting and crying all night long. I looked at him, gave him a kiss on his lips, said goodbye, and walked away.

Chapter 32

(Princess – Why is love so hard to find?)

Going home for the weekend wasn't what I had planned but it just happened at the very last minute. Since finding out my little sister was pregnant, I'd been keeping tabs on her. I never thought in a million years that I would be an auntie before becoming a mother. Palace was always the quiet one that always kept to herself. She made good grades and never got into in trouble. I'd always heard that you have to watch out for the quiet ones because they were the sneaky ones. I guess the people got that one right because Palace snuck that pregnancy right up under our noses.

I was keeping tabs on Palace through Grandma. Our relationship had gotten better and a lot stronger. When we were in my grandma's house, she had a mouth on her and we constantly fussed about little things. At first, I never really knew where she was coming from but now I knew just what that was all about. My grandma just wanted us to be the best for us. She wanted us to overcome the obstacles that got in our way.

I pulled up to my grandmother's house and I was so happy to see my family. The Pork and Beans Projects, not so much. I'd been gone almost a year and nothing had changed. There was trash everywhere, half-naked babies walking around with snotty noses, unfit mothers on their phones not paying attention to their children, and the drug dealers were still in the alley try to sell dope.

Before I hit the door, my wobbling sister came walking out. My baby sister was about five months and I was very proud of her. Palace was still going to school, had a good job making thirteen dollars an hour, had managed to get her a car, and was on the waiting list for an apartment outside of the Pork and Beans. She didn't talk about her baby's daddy much, and it was just fine being a single parent.

"Hey, baby momma, look at you. Palace, you are huge, girl!"

My sister hugged me tightly. "Whatever, girl. I was about to head out to Mr. Freeze's ice cream shop. Do you want to come? Grandma is in the house sleeping."

"Okay, let's ride. I hope you can drive, girl, because the last time I saw you in action, my car almost hit the stop sign!"

I had to tease my sister because when we were young, she couldn't even park a car. I checked out the new ride. She'd just gotten a 2015 Camry, all black with wood grain on the inside. It was nice and drove smooth as hell.

We pulled up to Mr. Freeze and I saw a lot of my old friends there. My homegirl Maria rushed me and gave me a hug. I had not seen or called her since I'd left for FSU. We talked about old times. She gave me her new number and I promised that I would do better at calling. Palace was at the register ordering her chocolate ice cream and a banana split with extra cherries and whipped cream. That baby had her eating crazy but it was funny to see my sister order so much. Before she got pregnant, she would always try to watch her weight, trying to keep her 112-pound figure. I was about to order something until we both heard someone laughing and giggling loud. When we turned around to see who it was and I could not believe my eyes.

There was the man that said that he would never hurt me or cheat on me. The same man that was laying in my bed last night getting my goods. The same man that had been blowing up my phone for the last three months to make sure that I wasn't cheating, but here he was with a another girl holding hands. My heart was literally breaking as I watched him walk in with a pregnant woman at that.

I looked at Palace and she had tears in her eyes. I wanted to console my sister but at the time, we were both mad at the world right now. I looked again at the sight in front of me and not only did I see Kareme, I saw Nicole hugged up with some dude. My sister was staring at her. I walked up to Kareme.

"So this how we're playing now?" I questioned him.

Kareme looked me up and down like I stank or something. "Do I know you or something?" he asked like he wasn't just in my bed a couple hours ago.

"Really, Kareme? You going to play me like that when just a couple hours ago, you were in my bed?"

"How the fuck does she know your name, Kareme? I knew you doing this bullshit again!" the pregnant girl was talking to him.

"Look, I don't know you and I wasn't with your ass last night. I'm not the type of nigga that would lie on my manhood so shorty, miss me with the bullshit that you are trying to pull. I think you are just trying to make my wife upset."

"Wife? Wife? Nigga, you married? I trusted your ass!" I was screaming to the top of my lungs. I looked at him and slapped the shit out of him before I walked to my sister's car. The pregnant girl was screaming all sort of whatnots to me but she wasn't ready for these hands. I had to walk off because I was seriously about to catch a charge.

Chapter 33

(Palace – Bitches and niggas ain't shit)

I could not believe my eyes. I swear bitches ain't shit. I saw Nicole, my best friend, hugged up with my baby's daddy. I knew she knew who Squeeze was. I had talked about this man multiple times to her. She knew how I felt about this man and the heartache and pain it caused for me every day to stay away from him. There was a part of me that wanted reach out to Squeeze about the baby, but the other half felt like I could do this by myself. It was better for me to raise my child in an environment that didn't concern any drugs or jail time. That was all I saw in Squeeze, a straight thug that didn't have anything going for himself. The way he carried himself told that story every day.

I walked up them both, not sure of what to say but it just came out."Really, Nicole and Squeeze? This is so low."

"Palace! Look at you! How many months are–" he was trying to ask but I cut him off.

"Don't act like you're all concerned now. You are up here hugged up with one of my EX best friends like you don't have a care in the world." I looked at Squeeze. "And for you, Nicole. I got you when I drop my baby because you knew all too well how I feel about this man. You played me big time but it's all good, boo."

I walked away with my head high. I was hurt but I wouldn't and couldn't let them see me sweat. When I got to the car, my sister was heartbroken and she looked like she had cried a river.

"Princess, I didn't know that the Kareme you were talking about was Squeeze's brother, girl. You should have saw his face when you slapped the shit out of him. Girl, his face was beet red like he was about to turn into one of my cherries on my banana split!"

My sister fell out laughing. I had to make a joke an out of this situation because that's exactly what this was, a joke. We left the parking laughing and cutting up. There was no need of crying over spilled milk.

Chapter 34

(Squeeze – Man oh man)

Seeing Palace with her perfectly round belly had me in my feelings. She was really pregnant, and the fact that the baby was mine had me feeling like a complete jackass. My grandmother told me that the reason for my sickness was because I had the morning sickness, not her. I never knew that the man could have the symptoms instead of the woman. Since my grandmother told me that, I had been kicking myself in the ass because of how I went off on her. I was missing out on everything. The doctor appointments, hearing my baby's heart beating, the cravings that she had... I was missing it all.

I had been trying for the longest to get info out of Pierre and Shuntae but their loyalty was with Palace. I had even went as far as asking the local drug boys about Palace. That's how I found that she stayed in the Pork and Beans with her grandmother. I went there a couple of times but her grandmother would always tell me that she wasn't home.

I never knew that about Pierre because our thing was strictly business. Pierre's business venture was about to blow up. Pierre wanted a better life for himself and his family. He was just as tired of the living situations of the young kids as I was. He was opening up a boys and girls club inside the Pork and Beans as well as two more inside the community. The deal Palace saw us was the night he was giving me some of his money for his part of the planning.

I was so much in my thoughts that I had forgotten all about Nicole being all up in my space. I'd met Nicole a while back at my grandmother's cookout. I thought she was all for Tres but about two months ago, my brother told me that she was just a friend from around the way. He wanted to hit but decided not to and went after Kashay's sister, Tara. I ran into Nicole at the gas station one day and we'd been kicking it ever since.

"So you knew who I was and you never once mentioned that you knew Palace?"

"What? I didn't know that was her, Squeeze, shit. Damn, don't act like that we have been together for almost two months now. Palace don't want to be with you anyway because she thinks that you are a straight up drug dealer."

"How didn't you know that I was the Squeeze she was talking about? Name another nigga named Squeeze that's around these parts, Nicole. Please tell me because I would like to know."

She had the closed mouth. She could not say nothing.

"Like I thought, you can't name one. Look, baby girl, you're cool and whatnot but that's not how I roll. I don't do friends, and damn sure won't mess with my baby momma's friend, period. How could you do that? That was your best friend, someone that trusted you, and loved you like a sister. Man, I got to go. You need to find you own way home."

I had to walk away from that broad fast. There was no way that I could stay around a chick that would degrade themselves enough to go after their best friend's baby's father. Now I had to get back in Palace's good graces. I hoped that it wasn't too late for me.

Chapter 35

(Nicole – Damn, Damn, Damn)

I saw Palace out the corner of my eye at the register and that's why I started to laugh loud enough to turn heads. I knew that she would see me with Squeeze, and that's what I wanted to happen. When she saw us, I saw the little tears forming in her eyes and I was proud of myself to be the one that was the cause of her tears. There were plenty of nights that I'd cried tears over her and Shuntae's friendship, so it was only right.

I had been dating Squeeze for two months and things were going great. I mean, he literally spoiled my ass. Whatever I wanted, I got. I thought that he was selling drugs, too, by the image that he portrayed but I was shocked when I found out all the things that his family did for the community. I would have never thought in my wildest dreams that a man of his image would be legal. That goes to say that you can't judge a book by its cover. At first, this was a revenge thing but the more I found about him, the revenge thing went out the window. I was falling for Squeeze and could see what Palace saw him the first place.

I knew after the episode that had just taken place with Palace that questions were going to be asked. I was prepared to answer them and thought that it would blow over. Squeeze and I had a good thing going. We really were feeling each other and I was in a relationship for once in my life. I had a man that cared for me and the feelings were real, and I'd messed that all up. I didn't think it would go down like that. I didn't know how much I'd actually messed up until he put it in perspective for me. I was wrong in every way. Not only did I lose a man that I cared for, but a friend that loved me unconditionally.

How could I be so stupid? Damn, damn, damn! Now I was regretting the whole thing.

Chapter 36

(Kareme – Married life and unfaithful)

I looked at Kashay in the passenger seat of our 2015 Cadillac Escalade. She was quiet and I could see she was more hurt than anything. Kashay and I had been married for four years and had one son named King, and a little girl on the way. I loved this woman more than life itself but for some reason, I'd always let my other head think for me and got me caught up in situations.

Since we'd been married, I had cheated on my wife five times, and Princess made it six. I'd met Princess at a frat party at FSU. I was only there because my frat buddy said that all the frat brothers needed to be there. My intention was meet with the frat and come home. I had just told my wife that side of me was gone and I wasn't going to cheat on her. Yet again, she had given me another chance. Kashay loved me through my flaws and all but this time I felt that she was done, and I couldn't have that. I couldn't let my wife walk out of my life. I didn't think I could live without her. She was like air I needed her to breathe.

Princess and I exchanged numbers the night at the frat party. I saw Princess moving her hips to the beat of the song and my manhood stood at attention. Princess was looking very sexy in her outfit and it was hugging every inch of her curves. I had to get in a dance with her but I never expected for me and her to go this far. We'd started calling each other and then we ended up having sex. Princess had me open, but I remembered that I had a family at home that needed me more than just a fling with a girl that was freshman in college. I'd graduated from FSU eight years ago. I was twenty-seven years old and Princess was just shy of her twentieth birthday.

I only slept with Princess last night because I wanted to end things but it didn't happen that way. I'd had to leave as soon as we finished having sex. Kashay had sent me a text saying that she was hungry for tacos and I had to make sure my wife and child were well taken care of. Now I wished that I could have had the opportunity to tell her because that one little mistake could have cost me my marriage.

Chapter 37

(Paris – Picking up the pieces)

It felt so good to drug free! I'd tried many times, but the devil was always busy with me. At first it was hard to kick the habit. The first couple weeks at the Kidaire Rehabilitation Center were the hardest in my life. The withdrawals I was having from the crack were worse than being in labor. Day in and day out, I was having night sweats, throwing up, diarrhea, and hot flashes. I never wanted to go through that again but it was all worth it now. I felt like I was reborn. I was glad that I had someone to go through the whole ordeal with me. Fletch had been there and now we were both clean and we had whole new outlook on life.

In our last of couple weeks there, the rehab coordinator helped Fletch and I get our own apartment and jobs. I was so grateful that I had a second chance at love and life. I had a lot of making up in my life and I wanted to show my kids that I had changed for the better. I had a grandbaby on the way. I could not have my grandbaby see me in the state that I was in.

Now that I was on to new things in my life, I had to get rid of the old. The day that I saw Prince Sr. was a bad day for me and would always give me a constant reminder of how bad the drugs had me. I saw he and that lady seemed happy, and I was now happy with my life with Fletcher. It was time for me to let him go, so I started off with filing for divorce from Prince Sr. Seeing him with her every day when I was hooked just made me indulge in drugs more than I ever would have. I wanted to not feel my heart breaking for the man that I loved so much. When I let crack go, I also let him go. It was better this way for me, him, and the kids.

I went to the courthouse with Fletch by my side. I walked in, went to the desk and asked what I had to do to file for a divorce. The young woman at the desk gave me the paperwork and told me what I needed to pay. I filed all the necessary paperwork but I didn't have an address for Prince Sr. When I went back up to the desk, I told the lady the situation. I gave her his full government name and behold, she found his address. It was a shock that he only stayed fifteen minutes from his children this whole time. I paid for my divorce and was out the door.

I had to make a stop at my mother's house. I hadn't seen her nor my children in three months. I could not wait for them to see my transformation. I pulled up to my mother's house and I took a look around. I didn't why but the sun seemed to be a lot brighter than I'd ever noticed. I knocked on my mother's door and waited for someone to answer the door. I knocked two more times and waited but no one ever came to the door. I thought that was weird because my mother was always home and barely went anywhere. I tried the door handle to see if the door was open because something just didn't feel right to me. To my surprise, the door was unlocked so let myself in my mother's apartment.

Once I got in the door, I got the shock of my life. All my children were there, along with my mom, and the screamed, "SURPRISE!"

I was so happy that everyone was there.

"How did y'all know?"

I looked at everyone and my mother came out and pointed to Fletch. That man was really my lifeline. He always kept a smile on my face. I looked at my baby and she had the prettiest baby bump that I had ever seen.

"Mom, you look so different and healthy!" Palace said to me.

Before I knew it, all four of my kids and had come up and gave me a group hug. When I looked at my kids, all of them were crying tears of joy. I looked at my mother in the background and she was holding on to her Bible and thanking GOD for bringing us all together in a blissful situation. We laughed, hugged, and cried and I was loving every minute of it.

Now it was time for me to give it to my kids straight. I needed to tell them the whole ordeal from how I got hooked on drugs to the point of me knowing where their father was. If I wanted to start over with my kids, they needed to know everything that I had been through. I didn't want to hide a thing from my kids.

When I finished telling the kids and my mother the scoop and what I been through, my kids looked at me and gave me a hug. I was grateful for the way it ended because I had my doubts about how the situation would end. I was more thankful that Fletch was with me through the whole situation. This was the beginning of something beautiful.

Chapter 38

(Pierre – No better time than present)

I was so happy to see my mother healthy and in good graces. My prayers had been answered. I'd listened to all my mother said and the thing that stuck out to me the most was that the man that was my father wasn't too far from us all this time. I really wouldn't have remembered how the man looked if I had not seen old pictures that my mom had. I still didn't know how he looked today. It was crazy what you could find out in an instant. My father was this close and I hadn't seen this man since I was one year old.

My mom had done some messed up things but she stuck in there, for a while, anyway. He didn't even try to come back. Now I knew his address so I had to make sure I made a stop by there, just to show him that I ended up doing well without him. I looked at my brother and he looked like he had something on his mind.

"What's up, brah? It looks something is on your mind heavy. Do you want to talk about it?"

"Pierre, he been here all along and he ain't reached out to us? Why, man, why?"

"I don't know, brah, but we will get our chance soon because we going to make a stop over there soon but right now, I have surprise for everybody." I had been waiting for months to surprise my family with what I had been working on. I couldn't wait until I saw my grandmother's face. "Hey, can I have everyone's attention please?"

Everybody was now looking at me now.

"For months now, I been putting a project together because I wanted better for everybody. I have been working under the table, helping with some construction jobs, saving money for something very special. The boys and girls club that you see being built in the Beans belongs to us, as in our family. I have two more throughout Florida. I'm tired of living like this, and Grandma, I bought you a new house."

I looked at Grandma and she fell down on her knees with her Bible in her hand, thanking GOD for everything. My granny deserved it.

She did so much in the community and she was everybody's granny. The community loved her and she loved everyone back in a major way. The looks on my brother and sister's faces were priceless. My mom was just smiling at me and I could not understand why.

"Mom, why you just smiling like that?"

"Because, baby, I was told long time ago that you was the one that would bring greatness to this family. I think back on it now and know that it was all true. I love you, Pierre."

That was the greatest gift ever. I hadn't heard my mom say those words in so long, it just made my day greater than before.

Chapter 39

(Sarafenia – Making good on his promises)

I was at work at The Rodeo. I was on stage doing my last number for the night. I was up on the pole moving my body to the rhythm of Busta Rhymes, and Niki Minaj's "Twerk It." I loved working the pole. It gave me a sense of feeling of being a free spirit. It was easy money and it was very refreshing for me.

I'd thought about quitting when my baby boy told me that I was about to be a grandma again. Now all my boys would all be fathers. But why would I stop what I loved doing? My kids were all grown, and I'd raised them. Now I was enjoying my life. I was finishing up my time on the pole when a gust of money was thrown at me. I looked to where the money was thrown from and I saw Mack standing up, smiling at me, showing me every last one of his gold teeth.

"I told you I was going to get you!" he said before pulling his shotgun from underneath his trench coat.

Everyone knew what time it was so everyone began to run. I got up and my mind was everywhere. I got up to run to the dressing room where I knew there was a back door. All I heard was shooting. I heard him coming through the back door and I ran around the corner. I was naked as the day I was born, with the exception of some fishnet stockings and some heels. I couldn't run to my car because my keys were inside the building.

Damn, I thought to myself.

I kicked off my shoes and began to run, trying to make it across the street into an alley. It was damn near three in the morning so the stores that were nearby were all closed. Just my luck. I was about to go into a dark alley to try to hide until I heard a horn blow, trying to get my attention.

I couldn't make out the face nor the car but at that point in time, I really didn't care. I just wanted to get the hell away. I jumped in the car and ducked down and we sped off. I didn't lift my head until he spoke.

"You can get up now. The coast is clear you can get up now."

I knew that voice all too well. I looked up the man that I hadn't seen in years. "Jamal, what in the world are you doing here?"

"It looks like I just saved your life, Nia."

I looked at Jamal for the first time in years and it was like he hadn't aged at all. He still looked good and his build was more muscular than I remembered.

"Jamal, I haven't seen you in years, and out of nowhere you're my knight in shining armor, saving me in the night?"

"Nia, I been to every one of your shows, I know all my grandkids, I know all my boys and I even know that Squeeze has a little one on the way."

"How is that you know all of that information?"

"Ever since the boys were young, I always kept up with them. I would have lunch with the boys at school. On their birthdays, we had a place that we would meet so I could give them their presents. On their birthdays, sometimes, or the next day after, I would take them out to get then a brand new toy or whatever they wanted. They would always tell you they found it or got it from a friend."

I looked at Jamal like he had lost his mind. I knew Tres, Kareme, and Squeeze would not keep anything like this from me, or would they? I thought so little of this man and even downplayed him from time to time in front of the kids. I did not want any parts of this man because of how he did me, and in a way, I took him away from my kids. But in fact, he'd kept in touch with them all along.

"I told the kids to always keep our meetings quiet. I knew you did not want to have any dealings with me and I wasn't going to let you stop me from seeing my kids. We tried that from time to time when I would take the time out to go to your front door. Every time, we would always fuss and almost fight in front of the kids and I didn't want my kids to always have that image in their head of me. That is why I started going around the kids the way I did. I know that I fucked up in the past. I'm truly sorry for the damage that I caused your heart."

I flipped the sun visor down and looked at myself in the mirror. Was I really that bad? I was hurting so bad that I'd really never looked at myself real good in the mirror. I tear stains on my face and I didn't have any clothes on. What in the world was I doing? I had no business being on nobody's pole when I was a mother and grandmother. I began to cry thinking my life was almost taken away from me because of a past mistake. Jamal made a bad mistake and corrected it in a major way, so why couldn't I?

"Don't worry, Nia. I got you. I'm here now and this time, I'm not going nowhere. You will have to kill me first."

I looked at this man and he put his hand on my knee. I could tell that his word was his bond. We pulled up to a nice brick home and I could tell it was a new construction.

"Who house is this?"

"It's mine, Nia."

He reached in the back and pulled out a coat and a blanket and wrapped it around me. After he made sure that I was wrapped up nicely, he got out and opened the door for me.

"Let's go in, Nia. We need to talk and you need to put on some clothes on."

We both fell out laughing and we headed inside the house.

Who says second chances can't have a happy ending?

Chapter 40

(Shuntae – It was just the simple things that count)

It was girls' day out and I was ready to hang with my girls. I hadn't been out with them in so long. On top of that, we were two weeks away from walking across the stage to receive our diplomas. Palace was now seven months pregnant but she looked like she was about to burst at any time. I'd been to all the doctor appointments with her. She didn't want to know the sex of the baby until we were all together, minus Nicole's trifling tail.

Palace, Brooke, and I all met up at the doctor's office. Palace's appointment was at ten o'clock. We had thirty minutes to spare to talk in the waiting room. We were all in high school but it wasn't the same as the past three years. All of our lives had changed in a major way, so the all the time that we used to hang out was cut short. We took extra classes for credits in our sophomore year so that our senior days in school would be short. We now only had to go three periods during the day instead of eight periods. The third lunch we used to have was no more. Our lives consisted of Palace, Brooke, and I going straight to work from school. The only thing that really bonded us to Brooke nowadays was the cell phone.

We were all sitting in the waiting area talking about all that was going on in each other's lives. Brooke finally admitted that she was completely over Peanut and she had a new boo. If there was one person that needed something new in their life, it was Brooke. She had been through so much with Peanut. It was past due for them to be over. I was so happy for my girl and could not wait to meet her new man.

Palace was still trying to convince us that she was good without Squeeze but we knew better than that. I knew my best friend and I tried to stay out of her and Squeeze's situation but she really needed him. He wasn't bad like she thought he was. In fact, he wasn't a drug dealer at all. He was a man of pride and with a loving heart who helped others. I tried to sugarcoat my telling her that she was completely wrong about him. Palace had her mind made up about him. I just hoped that one day they vould mend their situation for the sake of my niece or nephew.

The nurse called Palace and we headed to the back.

"Okay, Palace, we need to weigh you first, then take you temperature and blood pressure."

I'd been with Palace a million times to the doctor but it seemed like this was all new to Brooke. After the nurse took her vital signs, we headed to the ultrasound room to find out what Palace was having. We walked in the room and Palace got on the table, the doctor came in five minutes later.

"So today I finally get to reveal what you are having?" Doctor Williams was more excited than we were. She pulled up Palace's shirt and applied the gel to her stomach. She moved the wand all around, trying to locate the heart, then she looked for the baby's genitals. Brooke was gazing with tears in her eyes, she was truly amazed by what she was seeing,

"Okay, we are having–"

The doctor was interrupted with the opening of the door. We all looked to see who would be coming in now. Palace lifted her head, too, and it was Squeeze coming through the door. To say we were all shocked would be an understatement.

Chapter 41

(Squeeze – Listen up)

Pierre and I were completing the paperwork for the rec clubs that he had now. I didn't want to ask about Palace again because he never really gave me any info on his sister. This would be my last time trying, though.

"Pierre, man, what's going on with your sister, man? She is forever ducking me and I can't take it. That's my baby, too. I have a part in the baby, too. She can't keep shutting me out like this. My baby need to know who his or her father is."

I was all in my feelings. I'd been trying to get involved with Palace but it was like she knew that I was looking for her because she would never be in one place for long. I was tired and all I wanted was to be a part of her and our baby's life.

"Squeeze, man, I been trying to stay out of you and my sister situation. I know all too well how it feel to be without a father and that's not a good feeling at all. I've been trying to tell my sister that she should not judge a book by its cover. I don't why she thinks you are a drug dealer but she's dead wrong. The thing about Palace is that she is as stubborn as a mule. She's always been like that, even when we were kids. I know you are a good man, Squeeze. My sister has an appointment today at ten to find out what she is having. She is at the OBGYN on Main Street. Dr. Williams, my brother."

I swear that was the best news that I had heard in a while. I looked at watch and it was just after ten. I knew exactly where the doctor's office was. I rode past the office all the time. I was praying that I wasn't too late.

I pulled up to the office and I was a nervous wreck. I went to the receptionist and told her that I was looking for Palace Slain. She told me what room she was in and hit the lock switch to open the door to lead me back. When I got to the door, I heard the doctor about to reveal the sex of the baby and I could not let her say it without me being in there.

I walked in and all eyes were on me.

"You can go ahead, doctor. Sorry for interrupting."

She looked at Palace, making sure that it was okay to reveal the sex of the baby. Palace gave her a head nod to go on. I heard my baby's heartbeat filling the room and I began to cry. That was the sweetest sound I had ever heard in my life and it was something that I created. Another human being that was a part of me. Before I knew it, Shuntae and her other friend grabbed me and started to cry with me.

"Y'all got to stop. Y'all going to make me cry," the doctor said.

I couldn't stop if I tried. I was overcome with joy. I looked at Palace and she had tears running down the side of her face.

"Well, we are having a girl, ladies and gentleman!"

I was going to have a daughter and I couldn't have been happier. That only made me cry more, as well as the girls, too. The doctor came and gave me a hug and she, too, was crying by this time. Shuntae and her friend went and helped Palace up then showered her with hugs and kisses. They left the room to give us some privacy.

"What are you doing here, Squeeze?" Palace was still trying to be stubborn but I wasn't going to let that bother me today.

"What do you mean, what I am doing here? Palace, I'm a part of this baby, too. Whether you like or not, I'm going to be a part of you and our daughter's life."

Palace got up off the table and was headed straight to the door. "The hell if you are, Squeeze. What part of I don't want my child part of your lifestyle is it that you don't get?"

Before she could exit the building, the doctor called us both back inside.

"Palace, and I assume that you are the father."

"Yes, ma'am. You can call me Squeeze. That's if you don't mind the nickname."

"Okay, Mr. Squeeze, I'm going to need you to take Palace to the hospital and meet me there now."

I didn't even waste time after she said that. It was some kind of urgency in her voice and I wasn't taking any chances. I picked up Palace bridal style and took her to my truck. Her friends were still outside waiting.

"Hey, y'all, as you can see, your friend is not happy with me right now, and I really don't care. The doctor said that Palace needs to go to the hospital, now. I don't what the deal is yet. But I'm on the way now."

I hopped in the car and Palace was crying. I was scared to death because I didn't know what was going on but I had to stay calm in this situation.

Chapter 42

(Palace – A hard head make a soft behind)

I went to get an ultrasound and it was always a quick fix. I would get my pictures and be out the door. The fact that Squeeze came in caught me by surprise. I was shocked but on the inside, I was jumping for joy. I had mixed emotions. I didn't know if it just was me or if it was the baby making me act this way.

When Doctor Williams called me and Squeeze back, I thought it was because I forgot my ultrasound picture. I was in such a rush to get away from Squeeze that I totally forgot about the picture. When the doctor said that I needed to meet her at the hospital now, I wanted to fall right where I was standing. I was scared to death, prying that nothing wasn't wrong with my little girl. I was glad that Squeeze was there to pick me up and take me to the hospital because I really needed him now more than ever.

We pulled up to the hospital and Squeeze ran in and the nurse came with a wheelchair. Squeeze helped me out the car. The nurse wheeled me up to labor and delivery with Squeeze dead on her heels. The nurse got me settled in the room and hooked me up to an IV. The doctor still wasn't in and I was nervous wreck. Squeeze pulled up a chair and started rubbing my hand. I wanted to resist but I couldn't.

"Palace, I don't know what I have to do to get in your good graces. I apologize for coming at you the wrong way when you told me that you were pregnant. I was being a jerk, and I apologize from the bottom of my heart. The thing with Nicole, I swear I didn't know that y'all were friends. Those are lines that I don't cross, believe me. She did that on purpose. I guess it was plan to get you mad or something but I swear I didn't know and I hope you can forgive me for that."

I could tell that Squeeze was sincere with every word he spoke. He was just as scared as I was. It was written all over his face.

"I can forgive you, Squeeze, but I can't promise anything else. I can't get past the way you live. I can't be a part of that life and I won't subject our daughter to that either."

"What life is that, Palace?"

"The drug life that you live. I always heard how Squeeze was paid in the streets, then the night I saw you and Pierre in between the houses. The way you dress, sagging pants, Timberlands, wifebeaters sometimes. You dress like a straight up thug."

Squeeze was laughing at me hard. He was laughing at me so hard that he had started crying again. "Palace, you have no idea what you are talking about. I have never sold drugs a day in my life. As a matter of fact, I think drug dealers give Black men like myself a bad name. Have you ever thought about how your brother got his boys and girls clubs going? It was because of me. I helped Pierre get his dreams off the ground. What you saw in between those houses that night we met was Pierre giving me his part of the money so we could get started on his projects. Yeah, I have money. I can't lie. That's all because my grandfather and grandmother worked for it. The shelter you were working at, I own that one as well as two other ones on the Southside. I also own Restaurant Idella, named after my grandmother. The way I dress, well, that's just me. That's what I feel comfortable in, so I dress as I please."

I was feeling like a complete fool for all these months that I had been ducking and dodging and keep this man out of my life for nothing when he had a heart of gold. My hard head made for a soft ass. I felt so badly for the way I had been treating this man.

Doctor Williams finally walked in and I was happy to see her so we could find out what was going on with our little girl.

"Doctor, what's going on?"

"Palace, I asked you to meet me here because your sugar tests came back that your glucose is high, your blood pressure was sky high, and your amniotic sack is leaking a little bit. I need to keep you here until we can get this under control. You are thirty-three weeks along and we need you to make it to the full forty weeks. The baby right now is a little bit under the weight I would like her to be."

I was scared to death for real now. I had to call my mom and grandma to come to up here. I needed Squeeze but I need my nanna and mom with me also. Shuntae and Brooke were in the lobby and I was happy that I had friends that had my back regardless of anything. The doctor left and said that she was sending them in. I looked at Squeeze and he was trembling. His nerves were getting the best of him and he needed his nanna also.

Chapter 43

(Brooke – Best friends forever)

As I was sitting in the office with Palace and Shuntae, I could not wait to tell them all that had been going in my life. I didn't stay in the Beans nor did I ever have an absent parent in my life. In fact, my parents were still together and both were successful lawyers. I didn't live all fancy and didn't have all the finer things in life. I was the youngest of three kids but I was the only girl. My folks lived for my brothers, which made it hard for me. My brothers, Danny and Kris were a year apart and were now twenty-five and twenty-six. I was only eighteen. Since they were young, they'd stayed in trouble, in and out of jail for petty stuff like stealing when all they had to do was ask my folks for it.

My brothers felt that since our parents were lawyers, they could get out of every situation because Mom and Dad wouldn't let them see any jail time. Messing with them and their nonsense all the time left me lonely and numb. I didn't have parents that loved me and I wanted it so much. That's why in ninth grade, when I met Peanut, I fell so hard. He gave me all the attention that I needed and I fell head over heels in love with him. He was there when I needed him when my parents weren't. Three years I was with him, and every part of our relationship wasn't bad. There were a lot of good times. We both played our parts in doing bad, which eventually led Peanut to have a baby on me. Our relationship had run its course and to tell the truth, I was glad.

I was hoping that after we found out what the baby was, that Palace, Shuntae, and I would go somewhere to finish up our conversation. Palace had to be rushed to the hospital, so that was cut short. Shuntae and I were scared to death as we rushed to the hospital following Squeeze. I was glad that Squeeze came because he had every right to be there. I wished Nicole was there also so that we all could have heard the news together but Nicole had messed that up herself.

While waiting to find out what was going on with Palace, Shuntae and I said some prayers. We were waiting and praying that Palace and our goddaughter would be alright. We started talking and I needed to tell Shuntae and Palace both who the new love interest was in my life. Since Palace was in the back getting situated, I confided in Shuntae. I'd been hiding this from her long enough and it was time for her to find out.

"Shuntae, I need to tell you who I'm involved with now."

"Girl, who? Give me the scoop, child, and it better be someone fine, and someone that will treat you right because I don't mind handling somebody, girl. You know how I do."

I knew that Shuntae would be mad at me because my new boo was her brother, Danger. I knew the image he portrayed in the streets, and I knew that he was not to be messed with. But with me, he wasn't like that. He was the sweetest man. He was gentle, kind, and he expressed why he had the image he had in the streets. He told if me if you ever let someone get over on you or think you are soft, they will always take advantage of you. It happened to him before but it wouldn't happen again. When he was young, he was corner hustler, nickel and diming to make sure that he and Shuntae stayed with the freshest clothes and ate well. One day, he saw a girl, just thirteen years old, getting raped by man in the alley. He tried to help the girl by fighting the man and letting the girl make a run for it. The man pistol whipped him so bad that he had a broken nose, collar bone, five missing teeth, and he stole all his dope.

When he got healed up and back on the streets with bruises still visible, everyone thought that he was soft. So the local thugs tried him every way they could, and the only thing he could do was defend himself. He made a name for himself and it was Danger. All the people that tried him didn't mess with him anymore, either, because he used his hands to give a brutal beating or letting some shots off. He had to do whatever he needed to do to be safe in the streets. He was strict on his sister because she reminded him so much of the young girl that got raped. Shuntae was his little sister and his pride and joy. He would always be overprotective of her because he never wanted anything to happen to her.

"Well, Shuntae, my new boo is Danger."

"Danger who? Not my brother Danger. Girl, nah. This can't be right. You tripping, boo. You and Danger. I can't see that, Brooke."

"Shuntae, you may not want to believe it, but it's true. I'm in love with your brother."

Shuntae put her finger in her mouth like she was trying to throw up. I had to laugh at the girl because sometimes she could act like a true comedian. "I can't front. Lately my brother has been on his Ps and Qs and not acting so ratchet in the streets, so I guess that's got a lot to do with you. I kept asking him who his new boo was and he kept telling me in due time I would know. I'm happy for you and him. just don't hurt my brother. Y'all both deserve happiness in your lives because y'all be through too much not to be happy."

I was glad that Shuntae wasn't mad at me and that was a weight lifted off my shoulders.

The doctor came in and let us know that we could now go back to be with Palace. I was scared to go back because I didn't know what we would see once we got back there. Once she told us what the deal was, Shuntae and I were both wrecks but we knew we had to be strong for her. She wanted us to call her mom, grandma and Squeeze's grandma, and that's what we did.

Chapter 44

(Prince Jr. – Today was the day)

I woke up in my dorm room and realized today I was going to meet the man that I was named after. I hadn't seen him in years and today Pierre and I were going to finally come face to face with our father.

I got up and went to handle my hygiene before heading to pick Carmen up. I wasn't going to do this without her. I was going with Pierre but Carmen was the moral support that I needed. Since Carmen and I had been together, my life had changed for the better. Not only in my grades, but my performance on the field. I was now in the NFL draft. I was still going to finish college, of course, but going pro had been my dream forever. My favorite team was the Dallas Cowboys and I prayed every night that I got drafted to their team.

Carmen was staying at her sister's. I pulled up to her sister's house, honked the horn and my love came running out the house with a smile on her face.

"Hey, baby," she said to me and gave me a kiss with her juicy lips.

"Hey, love bug, you ready?"

"The question is are you ready? Prince, this is a huge step for you."

She was right. It was a very big step for me. My dad was my hero growing up and then one day, he was gone out of my life without so much as a goodbye. If he did, I didn't remember.

"I'm as ready as I will ever be, I guess."

I drove to the new boys and girls club that my bother owned now. I was proud of my brother. I always knew it wasn't just football he loved but he had a passion for helping others and loved kids. I pulled up and blew the horn and he came walking out with a suit and tie on with a briefcase in his hand.

"Cat daddy, look at you, man. Pierre, you look smooth, dude." I dapped my brother up and he got in the car.

"Thanks, man. I try. Plus, I had a couple of business meetings today so I to dress accordingly."

"Look at my brother the business man and in his sophomore year of high school, owns three boys and girls clubs. Brah, you the man."

"Nah, brah. You the man you about to go pro and a freshman at FSU. I can't top that."

We all fell out laughing.

We pulled up to the address that our mother gave us. The house looked like it was well kept and the grass was well-maintained. We all got out the car to approach the door. Carmen grabbed my hand as I prepared myself to knock on the door.

I knocked on the door and looked back at my brother who looked so confident in himself. The door opened and our father was standing there with a wifebeater and some jogging pants on.

"May I help you?" he asked with an uncertainty in his voice until he took a closer look at us. "Prince, is that you?" he asked me. I looked at this man and it was like he'd only aged five years. I would give him no more than that. He still looked like himself.

"Yes, it's me."

"Who do you have with you?"

"This is my girlfriend Carmen, and your son, Pierre."

He looked at Pierre and he shook his head.

"It's been so long that I didn't even recognize my own flesh and blood. How did you know where to find me? Let me guess, your mother told you."

"Yes, she did tell us where to find you. We really didn't come here for no pity party or anything. We just want to why. Why didn't you come see us, or even write? You were so close, only fifteen minutes from us. Not an hour drive or anything like that, only fifteen minutes and you couldn't take fifteen minutes out your busy schedule just to check on your four kids?" I was fire hot at this moment and the only thing that would calm me down was to hear his answer.

"Y'all don't understand the situation that went on between your mother and I."

"Come on, Pops. We know it all. Mom told us everything, and I mean everything. We even know how both of y'all got hooked on drugs, so please spare us the sob story," Pierre said to our father. Before I could get anything else out, Pierre had hit our father dead in the nose, making him fall in the doorway.

"I guess I deserved that," he said as was getting up off the ground.

"Look, I just came here to tell you this I came out good without you. I own three boys and girl clubs and I'm only a sophomore in high school. Palace is about to become a mother and her boyfriend has more money in the bank than ever. Not by selling drugs, and but helping others. Princess is studying at FSU to become a doctor. See, we all came out all right without you in our lives and there's no reason for you to come around now," Pierre said and walked back to the car.

"Prince, is that how you feel, too?"

"Look, I'm not as harsh as my brother but he has a point. I'm about to go pro and it's not because you were out in the yard playing catch with me. Mom may have got hooked on drugs and all but she loved us and groomed us to what we are today. She even got cleaned up and back to the state she was in once before. I will be forever your son but there is nothing that you can do for any of us now."

"Okay, if that's how y'all feel, then its only one thing left to do."

He went inside his house and came back with an envelope. We said our goodbyes and Carmen and I headed to the car.

"You good, brah?" I asked Pierre.

"Man, I feel great. Let's go get something to eat. I'm hungry."

Before I pulled off, I opened the envelope that our pops had handed me. It was the divorce papers that our mother had sent him. I guess that was his way of saying that he was divorcing all of us. I put my key in the ignition and was heading to get us all something to eat. I felt my phone vibrate in my pocket.

"Hello."

"Prince, this Shuntae. Palace is in the hospital and y'all need to get here."

"We're on our way," I told her

"Brah, who was that on the phone?" Pierre asked

"That was Shuntae. Palace is in the hospital and we need to get there."

I did a U-turn and headed to hospital to see what was going on with my baby sister.

Chapter 45

(Princess – The call)

I'd just finished my shift at the nursing home I was working at. Unique had gotten me a job working with her. I had to admit, I was loving every minute of it. It took my mind off the situation that happened with Kareem and me. I was hurt but realized I was better off single. I was better that way and my heart was safeguarded from any harm being done to it.

I was on my way to the dorm to get some rest. I didn't have any classes today. I was about call my mom but she was calling me instead.

"Mom, I was just about to call you."

"Princess, can you please come pick me, your grandma, and Fletch up, please?"

"Yeah, Mom. What's going on, is everything alright?'

"I don't know. I just got a call from Brooke saying that Palace was in the hospital. I'm a nervous wreck and I don't want to drive right now and Fletch don't want to drive with the state I'm in."

"I'm on the way, Mom. I will be there in the moment."

My mind was going everywhere. I praying that my sister was okay. I put my car in reverse and was headed to pick my mom, grandma and Fletch up.

Chapter 46

(Squeeze – Happy Happy)

I had never been this nervous and happy at the same time. Nervous because all that was going on. Happy because Palace had forgiven me and finally let me in her life. I could still hear my daughter's heartbeat throughout the room, as the nurse had her hooked up to the monitor and the sound was turned up so that I could hear her heartbeat. She had a strong one, too. My little girl was letting us know that she was going to be alright.

"Palace, have you thought about a name yet?"

"I was thinking about Davonia Nachell Bytiness. What you think?"

"I love it. Thank you for naming her after me." I looked up and I could tell Palace had some discomfort in her face. "Are you alright, Palace?"

"My stomach is hurting. Can you please go get the nurse?"

I ran to the desk to let the let the nurse know what was going on with Palace. As I was about to head back into the room, my granny, mom and pops came walking through the door. I was glad to see my mom and pops together. For years, my pops had made us promise to keep quiet about him being around me and my brothers. I was glad that it all finally come out.

"Squeeze, is everything okay?"

"Palace is hurting right now and I don't know why. The doctor said that her blood pressure was high along with her sugar, and something about her sack was leaking."

"Squeeze, can we go back with you?" my grandmother asked with a concerned look on her face.

"Sure, grandma. Come on."

When my grandmother walked in, she looked at Palace and gave her a forehead kiss. "Palace, baby, you are going to be alright, you and this baby. GOD got you both. Don't worry yourself." My grandma started praying and rubbing Palace's hand.

"Nice young woman, son. Y'all look cute together. I promise that I will be better than I was before," my mom said to me

"What do that mean, Mom?"

"Well, let's just say there will be no more pole for me. I took a real good look at myself, thanks to your father here. I'm a mother, and a grandma, I should carry myself as such."

I couldn't believe that my mother really was changing for the better. I was happy for her. I looked at Grandma and she winked her eye at me, letting me know that she approved.

Doctor Williams came back in the room with a crazy look on her face that I could not read.

"Well, I want our princess to stay in the oven a little while longer but she says she ready to get out of there," Doctor Williams said.

"What do mean by that, Doc?"

"Well, Squeeze, we need to do an emergency C-section to get her out of there. Palace's sugar is way too high and I can't risk the baby to a diabetic attack or even a coma to Palace's body."

I was really worried now because I really didn't know what to do. My grandma grabbed Palace's hand and mine, and put them together.

"GOD got something special planned for the three of you. Y'all was brought here today for a reason. I don't know if it's just the birth of the baby but it's something. I will say again, GOD has y'all in his hands."

Chapter 47

(Palace – Scared moment)

All of a sudden, I felt a sharp pain in my stomach and my head started pounding. I told Squeeze what was going on with me and he rushed to go get the nurse. I didn't know what it was but my daughter started kicking the mess out of me, like she was trying to bust her way out of my stomach.

When Squeeze came back, he had Ms. Idella and two other people. Ms. Idella came and gave me a kiss and was rubbing my hand. I loved that lady. she had such a heart of gold. Squeeze introduced me to his mother and father. I have seen his mother before but never dressed like she is today. She wore much revealing clothes when I used to see her at the shelter like she was trying to find her a Tender Roni .

When Doctor Williams came back in instead of the nurse I knew something was wrong. When she said that she had perform and emergency C-section. I knew what she meant. I had been reading pregnancy books every chance I got since I'd found out I was having a baby. I wasn't prepared today to have a baby. This was so unexpected and now I was going under the knife. where was my mother, granny, and sister when I needed them most? As soon as I had the thought, my mom, granny, Princess, and Fletch came walking in the door.

"What's going on, Palace? Is everything okay?" Granny rushed to me.

I started crying when I saw Grandmother and Mom walk in. "No, Granny. I'm going under the knife. They have to do an emergency C-section. My sugar is too high and they need to get her out now."

"Her? Her?" I hear my mom and sister shout.

"Yes, I'm having a girl."

My sister, mom, granny and Fletch all gave me a group hug. When they finished, everyone started to introduce themselves to each other.

"Idella, is that you?" Granny asked Squeeze's grandmother

"Pricilla, is that you?" Ms. Idella replied.

They both hugged each other for what seemed like forever.

"Y'all know each other?" I asked because I was dumbfounded for a minute, looking at the scene unfold in front of me.

"Girl, yes. I know your grandmother and been looking for her a while now. Your grandmother, Cassie, and I were best friends until the war moved us all to different areas of the country."

I looked at them both and I guessed that there was a reason for everything because we were one big happy family at the moment and it was all love.

"Okay, can everyone go inside the lobby except the ones that will be in the delivery room?"

The nurse asked me who I wanted in the room. I looked at my granny first.

"Girl, no. I have seen enough in my day. I will wait this one out."

Squeeze's Granny said the same thing.

"I guess it will be both of our moms," I told the nurse.

Everyone left and the four of us were there with the nurses preparing for the C-section. I was getting wheeled in another room when Doctor Williams came to me.

"Palace, I'm giving you something that will make you sleepy. By the time I count to ten, you should be out."

She began to count, and I only heard one and two before I was out.

Chapter 48

(Squeeze- Loving this moment for life)

I looked at Palace laid out on the table. This wasn't the image that I pictured it would be in a delivery room. I wanted to be holding Palace's hand as she called me all sort of names. I wanted to see my baby's head crowning in between her legs. This was the total opposite of what I ever imagined.

I looked at the doctor as she was cutting through the layers of skin to get to my daughter. I was amazed at what I was seeing. When she finished cutting the layers of skin, she used some instruments that looked like tongs to widen the entrance. She popped something and I saw a watery like substance flowing everywhere. I turned my head. I couldn't look at the rest until I heard faint little cries of my baby girl. I looked and she was prettiest sight that I could ever imagine. The doctor handed me a pair of scissors and I cut the umbilical cord that attached to my daughter to Palace.

"Would you like to hold your daughter now, Daddy?" the nurse asked me.

I was scared because she was tiny and I was scared that I was going to hurt her. Once I put her in my arms, she became quiet and I could hold on to this moment forever. I looked at Palace and she was coming out of the sleepy state that she was in.

"Is everything okay? Is she alright?" she was asking our moms.

They both shook their heads letting her know that she was okay.

I looked over at her and showed the precious jewel that we'd created.

"She is so beautiful in every way." I lowered the baby down enough so that Palace could place kisses on her. I looked at Palace and I placed a kiss on her lips then whispered in her ear., "This was a love worth fighting for."

Looking for a publishing home?

Royalty Publishing House, Where the Royals reside, is accepting submissions for writers in the urban fiction genre. If you're interested, submit the first 3-4 chapters with your synopsis to submissions@royaltypublishinghouse.com.

Check out our website for more information: www.royaltypublishinghouse.com.

Be sure to LIKE our Royalty Publishing House page on Facebook

CPSIA information can be obtained
at www.ICGtesting.com
Printed in the USA
LVOW13s1020100317

526787LV00009B/127/P